I0521426

Theaker's Quarterly Fiction #49

Edited by
Stephen Theaker
and John Greenwood

Theaker's Quarterly Fiction #49

Edited by
Stephen Theaker
and John Greenwood

Cover Artist

Howard Watts

Cover Model

Harriet Wakefield

Contributors

Tim Atkinson
Ross Gresham
Jacob Edwards
Rafe McGregor
Michael B. Tager
Douglas J. Ogurek
Antonella Coriander

ISBN (print): 978-1-910387-03-0

ISBN (epub): 978-1-910387-04-7

ISSN (print): 1747-6083

ISSN (online): 1747-6075

Website: www.theakersquarterly.blogspot.com

Email: theakersquarterlyfiction@gmail.com

Lulu Store: www.lulu.com/silveragebooks

Feedbooks: www.feedbooks.com/userbooks/tag/tqf

Submissions: Submissions are very welcome! See website for guidelines and terms.

Advertising: We welcome ad swaps with small press publishers and other creative types, and we'll run ads for relevant new projects from former contributors.

Sending material for review: We are interested in reviewing almost anything that's fantasy-related. We prefer to receive books for review in epub or mobi format. Feel free to send ebooks without querying first. We review about 10% of items received.

Mission statement: The primary goal of *Theaker's Quarterly Fiction* is to keep going. We need a new secondary goal.

Published in Theaker's Paperback Library on 14 November 2014.

Contents

Editorial

Fiction

Interview

The Quarterly Review

Reviews by Stephen Theaker, Jacob Edwards, Rafe McGregor, Tim Atkinson and Douglas J. Ogurek

CONTENTS

CONTENTS

Theaker's Shorterly Reviews

Stephen Theaker

Hi chums!

You may notice that my reviews for our blog and magazine, rarely very lengthy, get quite a bit shorter in future. It's not a general policy change at the zine. We're as happy as ever for reviewers to work at their own preferred length. It's just a change for me as a writer. I've been leaving a lot of reviews unfinished, because I don't have a lot of time to write, and it's been bugging me.

For one thing, the backlog has been a drag on my reading, because I don't want to start reading other books that are for review and thus add to the pile. And I think a timely hundred-word review is more use to everyone than a five hundred-word review that arrives three years after the book. I'll probably end up writing about the same amount in total, just spread across more items, and with reviews appearing more promptly.

As part of this change, I'm adding star ratings to my reviews. I know they're not universally popular, but if you're only writing a hundred words or two, a star rating saves a lot of time, saying quickly and clearly exactly how good you thought something was. I thought about returning to our old ten-point scale, but it doesn't have the equivalent of three stars, the perfect rating for something you liked just fine, but didn't adore.

Anyway, hope that's all okay. Just wanted to let you all know! Enjoy the issue!

Contributors

Antonella Coriander has (in this reality, at least) only ever been published in *Theaker's Quarterly Fiction*, to her great dismay. Her story in this issue is the third episode of her ongoing Oulippean serial.

Douglas J. Ogurek's work has appeared in the *BFS Journal*, *The Literary Review*, *Morpheus Tales*, *Gone Lawn*, and several anthologies. He lives in a Chicago suburb with the woman whose husband he is and their five pets. This time he reviews the film *Deliver Us from Evil*. His website: www.douglasjogurek.weebly.com.

Howard Watts is a writer, artist and composer living in Seaford who provides the cover art for this issue.

Jacob Edwards is a steward on Australia's speculative fiction flagship *Andromeda Spaceways Inflight Magazine*, but he moonlights with us when in port. This writer, poet and recovering lexiphanicist's website is at: www.jacobedwards.id.au. He also now has a Facebook page (www.facebook.com/pages/Jacob-Edwards/467957066679321), where he posts poems and the occasional oddity. He can be liked and followed. (More than that, he should be!) In this issue he reviews *The Making of Star Wars*.

Michael B. Tager's work has appeared in the *Atticus Review*, *Typehouse Literary Magazine*, *Schlock!* and *The Light Ekphrastic*. He likes Buffy, the Orioles and theatre. His debut appearance in the magazine is with a forty-page novella, "Nebuchadnezzar".

Rafe McGregor, absent from these pages for far too long, reviews *Mr Mercedes* and *The Spectral Link* in this issue. So good to have him back!

Ross Gresham teaches at the Air Force Academy in Colorado Springs. His stories have previously appeared in #34 ("Name the Planet"), #41 ("Milo Don't Count Coup"), #44 ("Milo on Fire"), and #46 ("Wild Seed"). "*Ut in Fumum!*" is I think the longest in the Milo and Marmite series yet. You're going to enjoy it!

Stephen Theaker is both human *and* dancer. Someone should tell The Killers that there's no need to choose. His reviews have also appeared in *Black Static*, *Interzone*, *Prism* and the *BFS Journal*. His hobbies include watching television and reading books. His ambition is to completely clear his backlog of reviews in TQF50.

Tim Atkinson lives, reads and works in the West Midlands. Sporadically he jots down thoughts about SFF and more at www.magpie-moth.blogspot.co.uk. In this issue he reviews *Infidel* by Kameron Hurley and *The Violent Century* by Lavie Tidhar.

Ut in Fumum!

Ross Gresham

Prologue

With my face pressed into the turf, I got a long, close look at each sprout and blade. "Marmite," I panted. "Look at this. Something unnatural about the grass."

"Our blood pumped on it is going to be unnatural. Where are the babes?"

"South-south east. Don't call them that. I tell you, check out this grass. It's screwy."

"Clear your head, bro. Bro bro bro. When this press rolls off. Bro, we're going to skip." Marmite breathed a gulp. "Did you see that claw? It grew out under her wrist. Like a bone spike." He whimpered and puffed. "Man oh man, serious press."

Yes it was. The "press" Marmite talked about was literal. Waves of artificial gravity rolled across this crazy planet. They pressed us into the soil at about four Gs, four times Earth's gravity, firm enough that inflating your chest was a conscious exercise.

One minute we were running for our lives, pursued by a hunting party of militant fox ladies. The next, gravity rolled in and brought us to the deck. *Whoof!* It was like being tackled by four big dudes, four big dudes who sat on your ribs.

The gravity stopped the fox ladies too. Down we all went. Chase suspended! Time out! The grasses bent and the bushes sagged and – *pop pop pop* – tree branches snapped, because four Gs was *heavy*, worse than usual. The hunt party had gone to ground about five hundred metres behind us.

Yip Yippee! Yip! They called the same thing, over and over again. They certainly didn't try to conceal their location, and the dense air carried their voices clearly, like music across a lake. The talk was incomprehensible but full of glee and giggles. It was easy to imagine a slumber party – teenage girls – touched with moonlight madness – time to pierce ears and squeal big secrets.

And why not? Why shouldn't they be pleased? They had two bad-ass soldiers running for their lives. And these beast ladies grew up with random gravity episodes. To them, this was just weather.

This shithole planet was called O'Malley's Emporium. (I know. Don't get me started.) It was an earth-furnished planet, standard terraforming package. With the pines and huckleberry bushes, Marmite and I could have been fleeing through a meadow of Yellowstone Park.

Which is why the grass was a puzzle. The gravity wave had slapped me down forward, prone, face in the dirt. I'd seen all these types of grasses before, and I was seeing them now. They were up my nose and picking my teeth. I'd breathed the same pulpy crush. But somehow they *looked* different. They marched in patterns in the twilight.

It's true that the light was unique. Now the evening was lit with the cold, pale glow of space burn. I was face down, but Marmite was face-up. On his back he could appreciate the streaks in the sky. O'Malley's gravity tricks made for one crazy light show. Anything orbiting the planet was clawed down to burn in the atmosphere, so it was the Northern Lights, the Southern Lights, every meteor shower of your life...

Marmite hummed. "Milo. Human urine... throw them off the scent."

"Marmite, they're in plain sight."

"I tried it anyhow. Bro, confuse pursuit."

Some fox ladies carried beam weapons. At any time during the chase they could have blasted off our legs. Instead they seemed bent on capture, which to you might seem to you like a merciful blessing. To me, the thought spurred terrified exertion to fill my lungs and speak: "Marmite. Love of god, if they catch us, don't talk anymore. Don't touch or look at them. Don't say anything or do anything. Promise me that. Love of god."

A crunching noise from afar, growing closer. The artificial gravity came in waves. You could see them and hear them, like a fat invisible baby rolling over the landscape. More trees popped. The wave hit us and Marmite grunted: "What, five Gs? O'Malley is really laying it on tonight."

The new surge pressed and released. "Can you flip? Look at this grass. Tell me what's wrong with what I'm seeing."

Marmite ignored me. "*That*'s why O'Malley is pumping the pedal. He caught a whole fleet. Like forty ships burning through the sky. He caught a cruiser. Looks like a Tony dreadnought. Man, we're going to have Tonies down here. Crazy fucks. Jumping around."

"A Tony ship? No. Please. It'll break apart."

"I don't see why. It's a lander."

O'Malley could multiply his planet's gravity. He lured craft into a comfortable orbit, then flipped a switch and pulled them down. He had all kinds of schemes to get visitors close. He advertised – brochures, coupons, fake distress beacons – and it was always a trap. Often he got whole ships down without breaking an egg. He got salvage and sometimes slaves.

There's a lot to tell. This is not a simple story. In the

end, I'm a brigadier general. That's right, I'm running the show. Marmite gets married for maybe the eighth time (without having annulled any previous covenants). But I can save time in one area: Malcolm O'Malley was a dick, a full-bore dick. Of that, never be in doubt.

All at once, the artificial gravity released. We were back to earth-normal, one G or a little less. I rocked to my feet. Oh man. Gradually my hams started to unlock, then my spine. The gravity waves had pounded every muscle like a sumo massage. "Let's clip! Marmite."

Marmite had rolled to all-fours. The seat of his pants was muddy with piss. His head hung down.

The distant yipping grew quieter, as gravity rolled off our pursuers. "Marmite. Their spears have far too many barbs for practical usage."

He studied the ground. "This grass. This grass. Milo, it's sharing."

"Sharing?" That was it. That was the oddity. The grasses swirled in shapes and patterns. Rows and lines. Most grass competes. This grass shared. It took turns.

Marmite's expression went from amazement to fear. Fox ladies rose all around us, in a silent circle. Marmite and I were in a ring of homemade spears. Each spear was tipped with a fan of points, and these points were stamped out of soft, salvage metal. Once these tines slid into your midriff, they would take new shapes. They were not coming back out without jerking and tearing.

These fox ladies themselves were different colours, dark and light, with the most beautiful fur. The most beautiful faces. Breathtaking. But they hated that they were beautiful, so they rubbed black clay into their faces, to shape their mouths into muzzles.

These particular scouts were naked. Their clothes

were torn and torn off. They were bleeding at the forearms and knees. While the main party hung back, making all the noise, these six had dragged themselves through the heavy gravity. Each had performed a feat like dragging a motorcar.

They had torn their skin and their clothes, and now they looked like a racy photo shoot. Girls in chains! Smudged and tattered, like a cheap tits-and-ass poster. I risked one pleading glance at Marmite. "Eyes up. Jesus. Eyes up."

Mildred stepped from behind. She had led them, of course. Her hair and fur were pressed completely flat, like she'd squeezed through a muddy culvert. She watched my eyes carefully. Daring me to look at her nakedness. She had been watching for that all along.

She was the youngest and strongest. Her eye patch had been torn off in the crawl. She was missing not just the eye but some bone in that region of her head, and shaved her hair back to expose this old wound.

I studied the scar, to keep my eyes from dropping. I didn't want to provoke her. As a side benefit I didn't want to see the bone spike that grew in and out of her elbow. Let her stick it in me, if that was to be my fate. She wasn't going to feint and tease.

Mildred waited for me to make a mistake, to gape at her naked form. When I didn't, and it was clear I wouldn't, she yawped with irritation. "Fea-east," she growled. Around her companions she liked to pretend that it was difficult for her to talk human. She worked her mouth and made the effort. "Feast now."

But you could see she didn't really feel it. She didn't believe it. Something stirred her mind, clouds of doubt. She dropped her head away and to the side. Unbelievable, but she was suddenly shy of her ugly scar.

She rubbed her own elbow, studying. Something was wrong with her murder spike. It wouldn't deploy.

It was a wicked brown colour, like an ancient bone from a mummy, but only a couple of centimetres emerged.

Around us, the spear ladies shifted uneasily in their circle. Mildred was their war chief, their blood drinker, the spirit of savage thirst. But now she shrank like the shy girl waiting at the edge of the school dance. Her battle crew was more shocked than I.

1.

Ut in Fumum.

Ut in Fumum. You see that on the battle flags for the Seventh Cavalry. It gets mistranslated as "Up in smoke," with "*Ut*" as a false cognate. Languages are tricky like that, with Latin no easier than the rest. You think you're telling an alien girl that you love her, when in fact you're giving a recipe for pan-fried squirrel. Along with this particular mistranslation comes the apocryphal story: that *Ut in Fumum* is a Roman war cry, from the Seventh Legion. (Thus the cry passed to us, the Seventh Cavalry, by process of numerology.) The myth suggests that the legionnaires had something they wanted to burn down, and I've seen artists' depictions of flaming elephants on the rampage. So maybe the Seventh Legion was burning that enemy city of Carthage.

But let me interrupt this flight of fancy to tell you a footnote of regimental history, actual history, Seventh Cavalry history. *Ut in Fumum...*

Marmite once held rank. That's right. He was promoted to sergeant major, and retained that title for some minutes. Actually, now that I think on it, was he Sergeant Major, or a real gold-leaf Major? An officer? You could check the records. I do remember that in anticipation of the promotion, there was a lot of play

on the title from me and his mates in the Seventh.
One moment Marmite was just an asshole, and now
suddenly he was to be a Major Asshole. From Jagoff to
a Major Jagoff. Puke to a Major Puke.

The military is like that, in that they adopt words
that already mean something else. There was a light
spy vehicle, already very unpopular because of its
uselessness, called the Sub-Pirax-Underplate-Monitor,
or *SPUMe*. Sure, they made guys drive it. "Man your
SPUMe!" came the announcement. The drivers would
hang their heads, load the pale vehicles into the
cylindrical launcher. For a while there was this
armoured battle suit they called the *Impact-Tor*. It was
super tight in the rear, and the guys had a funny
cowboy walk.

Anyway, Marmite's promotion was announced. He
was a combat hero. There was to be a ceremony, where
he got pinned like with a boutonnière, and awarded a
quantity of new stripes. These were arm stripes he was
supposed to sew onto his jacket. He was also to deliver
a speech to the troops.

What? That's right. Marmite was to address the
assembled troops. That was the plan printed on the
event program.

Once I confirmed, I rushed and reserved all the
tickets for the first eight rows, then began to scalp
these tickets for astronomical prices. I pocketed twelve
grand and could have doubled that if I'd thought
ahead. The price for some seats skyrocketed as they
sold and resold, the seats on the front right. In the
end, by the day of the Marmite's speech, they could
not be bought for love or money, literally priceless.
They gave an unobstructed view of the faces of the
visiting dignitaries and their spouses.

So the big day. The band did some anthems. General
Obor gave a little talk, which contained plenty of

howlers (how, as a boy, he learned to "examine himself") but really just whetted the appetite for the main event.

Marmite stepped to the microphone, his face shiny from nerves. It was like a battle sweat. The crowd jangled him mightily. Safe to assume, in all Marmite's life, up to that point, no one had thought to call him forward for public address. Now, two thousand people waited for his words.

He didn't know the relationship of the microphone to his face. He bobbed and weaved like it was an impediment, and the microphone moved on its suspension, maintaining its position like a piñata, or like the speed bag in a boxing gym. He took wet breaths, obscene in amplification. He began...

Marmite's promotion was for the bloody skirmish on Helicon 7. Helicon 7 was the major Frog moon, the only occupied moon around their home world, Oz.

We'd taken the place without much trouble, or we thought we had taken it. The situation was pretty much our usual: Any time there was a straight fight, we humans kicked alien ass. This was especially true for the Seventh Cavalry. Never had one unit kicked so much alien ass. I don't think that's in dispute.

But then we humans would contrive to cede any advantage we had gained. We won every battle but, overall, the war was about a draw.

On Helicon 7 we made our classic mistake. To humans, you take a planet when you take the surface of that planet. Sure, maybe a few bogies are hiding in the basement, but by and large human life is conducted under the sky.

Not so for a lot of weird alien races. These races had been digging around for millennia. Their creation myths have life *start* underground, then everybody migrates out when that prime space grew crowded.

Long story short, these older planets were some wormy apples. They were dug through and through. They were absolutely cut with tunnels and caverns – cities and even whole countries piled on one another in the dark.

The big Tony planet, Mike., was in fact more like a wasps' nest than an ant hill, in that it didn't exist until they built it of their secretions. That's right. Not completely, but hold your stomach. Wait until I tell you about invading that place! We humans land, kill some aliens, feel pretty smug. All the while we're walking around on the outside paper. Hey man, what's this buzzing under my boots?

Okay, that's a different fight, different story. Helicon 7 was a standard rock planet. Our invasion force landed and harvested the visible frogs. Killed millions of them, with almost no losses. In the Seventh Cavalry we had new scoop attachments to deal with the corpses. It was less a fight, more a sanitation mission.

We win. Haul. Party down... All the while, kilometres underground, resides a whole college of super frogs. Helicon 7 housed the largest population of super frogs ever assembled. It was their war college. These frogs were the truly dangerous ones, which you never saw but in ones and twos during the entire war. At this college, hundreds of them bathed in the artisanal waters, supposedly their origin waters, and mind-wrestled with one another to sharpen their skill set.

Then, Halloween night, they poured out of a tunnel and overran our camps. Our scouts proved as useful as ever. We were unprepared for any hostilities. Heavy armour had been disassembled for transport. We had only light armour, Baby Burpers, which are not that much better than a jeep with thick windows. We were in costume.

It was a hellish scene. Just a Halloween party with

the Seventh is a hellish scene. Now Frogs were among us, and guys' heads started exploding. A man's head might explode, or he might walk up to you and blow *your* brains out with his pistol. Best friends put grenades down the back of each other's' shirts, like a prank with an ice cube.

Frogs hadn't fought a war in a long time, and in general their war methods were laughable. But special frogs had luminescent gills along their soft skulls. They controlled their fellow frogs, and this same ability allowed them to crawl into your mind and suggest bad decisions, like to kill yourself or your mates. If these frogs exerted themselves, they could also simply pull your plug. A gill Frog could sneak into a human mind and yank the power cord. When that happened, the man's face swelled out. Either the skull burst or there was an overflow from every valve hole. Eyes, ears, nose, and throat – *sploosh!* – the pot boiled over.

This happened right in front of me. I was wearing my Roman emperor costume, with a crown of laurels. A driver by the name of Poqueep stumbled up. Drunk? Of course, but he seemed particularly unsteady. "Don't barf, don't barf," I said, skipping away.

Whoop. His brain flopped out at my feet. His corpse toppled, and there stood a frog with those slick, electric gills. It took me another second to realise it wasn't some joker in a perverted Halloween costume, with batteries in the mask, and that we were all going to die. The frog reached out, and I felt that familiar contraction on the lining of my brain...

Blam! Marmite was atop our Baby Burper. He manned the swivel gun. He was wearing his gorilla mask, held in place with an elastic cord across the back. He shot that Frog in front of me. Then he began to kill them all, every mother's son.

Here's the thing. This was a victory party. This was a
Seventh Cavalry party. How can I explain... a Seventh
Cavalry party.

No officers allowed, of course. We'd shipped all the
commissioned officers off, first thing, with an easy
two-prong strategy. One, we exaggerated the work to
be done, the grotesque labour of the corpse disposal.
We vented an incinerator into the ducts of the officer
quarters. That was part one. Then, part two, we spun a
tale of perks available in the orbiting transports. The
transports were arriving to take us to the next fight,
and it wasn't hard to conjure visions of the luxuries
available. Lobster tails and umbrella drinks. Amateur
theatricals, with cross-dressing roles available and
even obligatory, given the gender imbalance. Soon
there wasn't a lieutenant left on the planet's surface.

A Seventh Cavalry party, okay? As a result, on the
night of the attack, Marmite was baked out of his
mind. Now, I'm not sure I can convey to you what this
means. Marmite can smoke vast quantities of weed
without any difference in the things he says or does. So
when I tell you that he was baked, I'm talking a unique
mental state, a third state spoken of in some religions.

Between the two of us, we had smoked a bale of
prime ganja. I was seeing the world through a
kaleidoscope. Then alarms going off, out of time with
the music but otherwise indistinguishable... tracer
rounds... Poqueep's brains on my shoes... electric Frog.
When I realised some of what was happening, I yelled
at Marmite to save himself. Get inside the Burper, fool!
Close the hatch! He yelled back saying he couldn't,
there were otters swimming around down there, and
he thought they would be mean to him. He swivelled
the gun, blasted a row of super Frogs.

Of course, our vehicle was the epicentre of the party.
That's a given. Milo and Marmite, Burper Team One.
We were at the top of a rise, under some strobes we'd

rigged. There was Marmite, spinning in the gun turret, a four-metre flame lancing out of the barrel, this crazy ape, snow-white hair coming out over the top of his mask... He was like a beacon for all available Frogs.

All at once, every Frog in the area devoted attention to him. He was the only danger they could detect, and Frogs could coordinate. *En masse*, they slipped inside his mind.

That was their mistake. I smoke, you smoke... Frogs had never smoked before. And now they went into Marmite's skull, and *kablam!* They were newbies, virgins. It was too much. *The experience baked the master Frog consciousness.*

After that, the fight was not much of fight. These Frog Overlords wandered off in search of snacks, or to tell each other profound thoughts. Marmite's gun sliced them down.

One other thing. This is important. Frog aliens – they have blood or some comparable fluid, but it doesn't circulate. Their anatomy is solid state, you know? With our human bodies, we ebb and flow. We pass from condition to condition. If you get sick, your body eventually sluices out the bugs. If you get drunk, you sleep it off. You get stoned, you drink some litres, take a nap, wake up tomorrow a little sensitive to sunlight, ready to fire the pipe if the occasion demands.

But once Frogs were high, they stayed high. Weeks later we'd still discover gill frogs wandering around. If they had time to get in your head, they didn't try to kill you. They just wanted to show you something cool.

After a few incomprehensible words, Marmite broke off his address to the crowd, provoked by the hovering microphone. He expected that he should hold the microphone, in the manner of music performances he had seen, but the microphone itself was programmed to allow hands-free amplification, so it would pull out of reach. Finally Marmite crouched, baited it close, then leapt. The suspension wasn't fast enough. He had it, and whipped the wire, like breaking the neck of a snake, to punish his defeated foe.

"Right, top cock on top," he muttered. The amplified sound made him jump back. "Oh yeah. Festival crowd. The Seventh. The Seventh. How's this? Top cock on top."

I watched from a first row seat. Marmite's eyes tightened, and dangerous colour suffused his face. At once, fear of crowds receded, to be replaced with maniac enthusiasm, the madness of a bonfire rally. "Top cock!" He did some shout-outs.

From the review stand, positioned at the rear of the stage, General Obor hissed something to his executive officer. This drew Marmite's attention. For the first time he held the microphone at the correct distance from his mouth. He propositioned General Obor's wife, bluntly, as though consent were assumed.

The General's Executive Officer ducked off stage, and made it to the power supply before anyone from the Seventh could stop him. I should have anticipated and secured all vulnerabilities. In the end, we only got seven profound sentences.

"New rules around here. Top cock on top. Right? First, get your smoke on. Got that, Seventh? In all situations that's the truth. First, get your smoke on."

You still sometimes see it on the older battle flags. "*Ut in Funum*". A Latin rendering. First, get your smoke on.

2.

Some months later, on like our ninth briefing on the invasion of Mikel, the Tony home world, and Captain Philippe finally got to the meat of the nut:

"...in accommodation of what may be fragile ground structures, care will be taken, with an eye towards eventual cessation of hostilities, to limit the use of vehicles that demonstrate little regard for the environmental and cultural sensitivities... instead the situationally-appropriate support of the SPUMe fighting frame with..."

"Oh Christ," I let out. All around me was the same. Exclamations. Primal curses. Translation? We were landing on Mikel with only light armour. We would leave our unstoppable tanks, the Big Burpers, on their specialized transport ships.

At this interruption, Captain Philippe set his mouth. He looked to his sergeant, blaming him for this failure to maintain discipline. Sergeant Yangtze wasn't happy with us, but he merely waited for the worst of the murmurs to bubble out. He understood: club a man in the belly, naturally he makes a sound.

Captain Philippe waited for the stern reprimand, however, or he had lost his place in his notes, or anyway he declined to continue. The Sergeant stepped forward. He waved his hand to the projector: "Listen up, meat. This is a Tony. This is the enemy."

"I'm going to be sick," I whispered. Marmite was there beside me. The Tony picture went through its motions, the strange, inefficient Tony dance that they did even when they were standing still. It was efficient for one thing: it cued every fear I've ever had. It lit up every hidden nook of my spine.

"...Vulnerable zones. We call these False Vulnerable Zones™. Because they are not Real Vulnerable Zones™. That's a difference you're responsible for. Meat, this is Top Secret Science, and we've been authorized to give it to you. We have labelled the False Vulnerable Zones™ here..."

The picture Tony was missing a leg at the hip. It didn't care. It smiled. A light moan arose from our group, generally, and my mouth was awash with stomach acid. We'd all killed plenty of Tonies. They only stopped twitching with complete disassembly.

The Captain joined back in, with some charts of Tony formations. The Tonies fought in sixes. Six was the important number for their species, and they had all these patterns of twos and threes.

"Marmite, do you have any pills or anything?"

He smiled absently. For all briefings he went into a meditative state.

"C'mon, I'm serious."

The whole situation brought you low. Captain Philippe's Xs and Os bore as much resemblance to a true Tony Six as a twelve-year-old's account of sex with his babysitter. The Seventh Cavalry was going into Mikel. We were going in with light armour, and we were going in with this guy. Let's face it. Even if we did everything right, plenty of us would be dined upon.

Sergeant Yangtze took the reins. "Listen up, meat..." More charts.

I hated him just as bad as Captain Philippe, maybe worse. There was nothing funny about Sergeant Yangtze. Captain Philippe was an ass clown – undeniable – everyone saw it first thing. In contrast, Sergeant Yangtze was serious. Took this seriously. He was right. He was right about where to shoot a Tony, and he was right that these were the Tony tactics: six-creature patterns, leapfrogging each other. That's how they would do it. You couldn't analyze them any better.

Yet at the same time, Sergeant Yangtze was just as wrong, and about everything. He was wrong that this briefing would change what was ahead.

Up front, Captain Philippe muscled back to the podium. An interplay had developed between the two men. The Sergeant said things that were real and true. He was a typical blunt sergeant, and took comfort in that role, in fact overdoing it, because everyone already knew all of the things he had to say, yet he presented each as a revelation.

The Captain had different a complaint. He was offended by straight talk, by its very nature. It didn't matter so much what was said. Plain statements offended him.

Most officers are like that. It's a matter of control. For true control – if the Captain really was in charge – then he could also control what was true. To just blurt the truth, fling it about... that was a challenge to his pre-eminence.

Try it sometime. Walk up to an officer and say some blunt, obvious thing: "It's cold outside." Watch his face, as this lands like a bad oyster – mouth tightens – unhappiness – peevish – time to correct the tuck of your shirt.

Also – to be fair – officers got pressure from above. When Captain Philippe left this briefing, he would go talk to other Captains, or Majors, or higher ranks. They had their own coffee club, and up there, the air was clouded by what they *wanted* to be true. There was a certain accepted picture. It was a picture of sure victories, and enthusiastic troops, all backed as one by a united citizenry joined in patriotic song... They had to believe that kind of thing, as the first requirement for membership.

Then the disconnect from reality ripped their brains in half. It made them all insane.

Brother. Who cares. All this is by the way. A little tilt-and-lance between a bullet-headed sergeant and a huffy Captain, giving himself the vapours.

I had my own concerns. I was puking into my mouth and swallowing it down again. The briefing continued. Blue dots made war on red dots. Attack and defence. None of it bore relation to the mad, howling mad rush of a Tony fight. A Tony would change trajectory in the middle of a leap. I know that's impossible, but so is everything about them. Their unnatural joints and bends... Their speed, like a broken movie skipping frames... Their body fluids etching obscene designs on your periscope glass...

There was no elation in killing a Tony. Take a moment and imagine that. Tonies were as terrible dead as they were alive. I hated those creatures. They were the only thing I've ever hated. I didn't even want to kill them. I just never wanted to see one again.

I was going to faint. I did sort of faint. I fainted into my hands, sitting there.

"Buck up, squire," Marmite said.

"I'm going to hang myself."

"Wait for it."

"Wait for what?"

Marmite smiled and sat complacent.

A moment later, this was explained. Sergeant Yangtze called, "Volunteer units fall out. Milo. Marmite."

My organs began to die, one by one. I misunderstood that Marmite and I were reconnaissance scouts. The sergeant had said something about reconnaissance scouts. Request for volunteers. They couldn't even get *androids* to land as reconnaissance scouts, not on Mikel, not without stripping half their brain circuits.

"Got us on a special mission." Marmite savoured the victory.

"Please no..."

"Pulled rank. That's right. Top cock on top."

"Pulled rank?"

Rank, to Marmite... he didn't understand that he no longer held rank. In his locker he kept some of the stripes and badges they'd awarded him, like a magic totem. He hid these insignia in a pill box. Until our superiors discovered and physically took them back,

Marmite felt that he retained his full powers and authority.

"Li-ai-son." Marmite stretched the word to savour it.

"With the fucking Tonies...?"

"O'Malley's Emporium," he said, under his voice. The Sergeant and Captain were up with us. It was the first I'd heard of the place, or the name. Marmite winked to me. "It's a planet."

About then I began to understand. Marmite had gotten us out of the Mikel invasion. He had gotten us a different mission instead. I was saved. The first flush of relief came with the Captain, at my one side, consoling me for missing the action ("...operational situational requirements..."). The Sergeant was gruffer: "HQ needs two meats..."

Between them, Marmite wore his church face. Except he'd never been to church. He wore an unfocused gaze at the rafters, and a fat-lipped smile that would have fooled no one. That made you want to kill him, really.

A moment before, I would have traded anything to skip the invasion. Paid any price, sacrificed any limb, bolted down any hole. But seeing Marmite's church face, I was suddenly torn. I was being saved, yes, but I was being saved by a scheme of Marmite's.

I studied the Sergeant, the only possible reliable tell, but I got nothing. He was a straight talker, but it's not like he understood much. In another week he would be just another one of twenty-one thousand dead men. Dead? They were strewn apart. The first invasion of Mikel was not a success. We provided the Tonies with enough bio-matter that they secreted an extension layer on their planet.

3.

Our pod crash-landed on O'Malley's Emporium. It was chaos on the way down. The freak gravity played hell on the craft's systems, igniting counter-thrusters at random, flipping us end over end, then spinning us like a drill bit. Chutes shrieked out early and late, yanked out of their bolts or gone in a puff of black ash, *poof!*

A thousand metres before we hit the surface, the gyros got their head and fired the crack-back rockets, so we didn't crater. Instead we landed with a gentle *squoosh*, as on a pillow. The landing gear, baffled, had deployed five kilometres up, and the melting legs relaxed under the impact.

Those three minutes knocked me silly. My blood had centrifuged to places it didn't belong, the outer territories of my body. "Brother." I felt that I deserved a few moments to get my bearings, but the pod was a wreck, every light screaming, hoses flopping, and a jet of freon trying to freeze my nuts. "Brother." I flopped out of my rack, groaning. "Ay ay!" The floor was hot as a skillet. We had almost melted through.

"Hurry up, shitbag!" Marmite kicked the hull, *bong, bong, bong.* "Get in here! Cut the window!"

It's true that there were already sounds of rescue, outside the pod. So that was good news. Help was at hand, to extricate us from the wreckage. A torch buzzed and sparked on the outside of the hull, and over all the alarm noise – bizarrely – came the soft notes of an old stevedore robot. Their song is the airy notes of a calliope. That really was old technology, for communication between workshop components. They'd sing to coordinate a harmony for a particular process.

"Yo! Cut the window!" Marmite shouted at the rescue robot.

What made him mad was that one of our marines was dying. We had four marines aboard in their pressure tanks. Three slept on, drugged, but one was thrashing and convulsing, banging around in her tank, which of course was sealed.

Marmite pried off the panel. By that time I was over beside him and we shared a hopeless look. Inside, the medication governor was melted to goop. It would take us half an hour to jerry-rig a replacement, and god knows what was being pumped into her blood.

Marmite and I should have been asleep as well, because that was landing protocol. But one thing you learn in the Seventh is to land live. Stay awake. Half that shit they jam in your arm, you couldn't buy on the street at Mayfair. The rest of it, you're better off selling on the street yourself. Sneak the major needle out of your vein and stick it in a juice bag. I mean, first drink the apple juice, then put the needle through the straw hole, collect the dose. Some places, if you found the right buyer, you fund your whole holiday, 48-hour pass, 100 drinks, drinking top-shelf.

This time there hadn't been a chance to drink the apple juice. We were on a peaceful preliminary orbit when alarms started going off. We stumbled to our individual pods, and the artificial gravity tore the landing unit away from the ambassador's quarters. As the coupling broke, and the ambassador stood braced there in the open hatch before she was sucked, tumbling, into space.

That picture filled my brain. Then *zing!* I felt the stab, my machine tried to inject me. I yanked the needles out, and they pumped their sticky mess all over my forearm.

The torch continued to touch here and there on the

hull, indecisive, like two kids, first time, trying to play
at sex. (That's right, son, she doesn't want her ear in
your mouth.) All the while, the robot sang its happy
carnival notes.

Marmite left the dying marine. Somehow he primed
the door charge. "All right, sparky, stand clear." He
blew it out.

In the dust and sunlight, the robot snaked its neck
in. Ran its laser thread over everything.

Then it heaved itself through. The bot was a serious
piece of machinery, definitely, the chassis maybe a
century old, hung with different generations of
components. Slack-bodied, with that metal
Sharkskin™. Two discrete, roaming eyes and four
pickers, not counting the little legs. It was big, total
mass of a passenger car, took up all of the floor space.

Marmite danced to put his face right in one of the
eyes. "Medical team. Whatever you've got, send them
in."

Instead, one of the pickers flicked out a blade, sliced
open a carton lashed to the wall. It was a case of
Ambassador gifts, so all kinds of crap spilled out.
Gilded vases, lead crystal... an embarrassing array, but I
suppose ambassadors don't know how sophisticated a
culture they were going to interact with. This was
basically a box of mirrors and feathers.

Instead of recoiling, the bot poked into the case to
see the rest.

Marmite said, "What does it want with that shit?"

"I don't know. It's probably directed by remote. Hey!
Hey! Can you torch this open?" The marine had quit
kicking in her coffin.

The bot held a document with an embossed golden
seal. Some kind of treaty document, or letter of
greetings. It spent a long moment evaluating the gold

seal, the rest of the document coming apart in its metal grip, unregarded.

"Hey. Leave that worthless shit alone. Does your doc have flash-transfusion?"

By now it was clear that the bot didn't regard the human voice. I'd worked with these old nogs, though, in a motorcycle shop. I whistled a combination. It meant, basically, "over here, idiot".

The robot slithered. It put an eye over the marine's case, and shoved a picker into the panel hole. Immediately, up popped the lid.

The marine inside was yellow, mustard yellow. She was dying. Big, solid, older lady. You could smell from the steam that her insides were ruined. "She needs a total flush," I said quietly, not much hope, but maybe there was a human watching at the other end of the robot eye.

The robot offered her handcuffs.

It took me a minute to get what they were. Handcuffs. They were handcuffs with the collar attachment. Dangling over the case.

The marine jerked once, cardiac arrest. At this point it must have been like her fifth heart attack, because her internal starter was out of battery. Really there was nothing to be done.

The bot was insistent with his little collar business.

"She's dying." I whistled a four-note tune, basically, fuck off.

The bot ignored me. A band of red lights marched around its centre. It was talking now, a sound recording. The voice was muddled with static, and I didn't speak the lingo.

The bot raised a picker high, poised, like a scorpion's tail, then *thung!* It put its spike through the marine's body. Right through. It pinned her dying body to the bed. She convulsed around the pivot point.

"What the...?" Marmite launched into the bot and

bounced off. The violence got the robot's attention. An eye snaked around. The picker offered him the same cuffs and collar. The spike pulled out of the dead marine. It arced and tensed like a spring over Marmite, dripping gore.

I whistled warning notes. *Look out!* This overrode any protocol in the bot brain, and the sensors returned to me. From behind, Marmite leapt and hugged the spike arm to one of the idle pickers.

This hug drove the bot crazy. It turned and undulated and flopped against the wall, and Marmite rode with it. The picker with the cuffs dropped them, and all four arms flicked out blade attachments. It was a knife fight in a phone booth with a four-armed metal squid.

Knife fight? Maybe it thought so. Like most crazy marines, the dead one kept her sidearm with her, even asleep. It was coded to her, so I used her bloody hand to draw it from her chest scabbard. Luckily her body temperature hadn't cooled enough to disable the weapon. *Blat! Blat! Blat!* I put three slugs through Sharkskin™, high, middle and low. They were digger slugs. They knew where to go and what to do. *Pop! Pop!* the skin bulged out as they roamed and delivered their explosive payloads.

Everything was still. One nice thing about bots is that when they die, they stiffen and relax. They don't spasm when dying, like live things. The bot settled to the floor like a beanbag.

Marmite grabbed the slack, dying eye, and pressed something to it. It was crossed sabres, the insignia for the Seventh Cavalry, which he'd ripped off his uniform. "Call your boss," he said. "Yo, check this." He rubbed it on the lens. "That's right. The Seventh. Read 'em and weep. *Ut in Fumum*. You just fucked with the Seventh Cavalry."

The other marine ladies were fine, vitals okay, dreaming their druggy dreams. Their call signs were stencilled on their cases. Pembroke, Manfred, and Geppetto. There was no way to wake them today, but I started the process with the override levers. It would be twelve hours until they could open their eyes, sixteen until they could jog.

Marmite worked on the dead bot. "Why did it go for her first?"

"Must have a thing for women."

"It wanted a girlfriend or something? Man, we're fucked. These little bitty legs. This boy didn't walk. It has a ride out there."

"Yep."

We checked the marine weapons. Obviously they were coded to the individual, and marine weapons were famously recalcitrant. As with marines themselves, you could waste all year trying to change the mind of a marine rifle. There also a few scattered grenades, but trying to re-permission a marine grenade was an existential act.

One of the scattered ambassador gifts actually was a hand mirror. I raised it out of the hatch to give me a glimpse of the world, like a periscope. "Marmite, what is this shithole place?" It was empty plain covered with wrecks. Space wrecks, everywhere. It was a graveyard of wrecked spacecraft, of every sort: Human, Frog, Capo, Tony. Some I didn't recognise. "O'Malley's Emporium?"

Sure enough, a large robot hauler idled beside our craft. It held another three robots like the one we'd just trashed. I could hear them starting to communicate, singing interrogative notes. *Dootle-y-do?*

"All bots," I reported.

"Split up, then. Perpendicular vector." He looked to

the sealed marines. "If we get far enough it'll forget the pod. Maybe they'll get time to wake up."

"Okay, go."

"Wait." Marmite knelt again. He detached the ID plate from the dead bot. Its licence plate. Secured it in his waistband. He was serious about tracking it home, apparently. "On three," he said. "One, two..."

I dodged around for about three hundred metres before they caught up. I was dodging in and out of a maze of wrecks. I don't know how far Marmite got but he was already trussed and collared when they hauled me up by my legs. Based on Marmite's cursing, the machine had calibrated our language. "You are the salvage property of O'Malley's Emporium."

4.

"You are the salvage property of O'Malley's Emporium. Acknowledge your property status."

Marmite groaned at the repetition. His head had been bashed during capture. Blood stained his white hair the colour of carrots.

We were in a trailer for preliminary processing, loosely tethered to two of the dozen seats, a dozen seats in two rows, like a briefing theatre. Other creatures had been kept here, because the room stunk of their secretions. For sure I smelled Frog. Out the greasy window was a trash and salvage operation, with different metals going into different recycling chutes. No people to be seen, yet, just robots and mud.

Our companion was a low, spindly-leg bot with five good legs and one lame. All its joints were squeaky, metal on metal, which had probably retired it from the salvage fields.

"You are the salvage property of O'Malley's Emporium. Acknowledge your property status."

"Yo, Ichabod," I finally said. "File your claim with the feds. The man and I already sold our souls. You'll find that we signed papers for the Seventh. That's right. The Seventh Cavalry, eight-year enlistment. So unless you want us to drop our Burpers down here, polish this whole fucking ball like a hot Zamboni..."

At least I changed the script. "Your debt for entry may be satisfied by..."

"Whoa, whoa," Marmite roused and plucked his own cuff. "What you have here is Burper Team One. Don't mistake all this chords and piping, all right? Thinking we're here to escort you to Prom. These are just dress uniforms. They made us wear them for protocol. We're an ambassador mission but our ship crashed."

The robot paused, as though maybe this message was being relayed. Marmite was instantly mollified. "All right. One, cuffs off, and cut the leash. Two, we need a ride. Whatever it is, my man here can drive it. Three, we need some drinks. And four, we need some hospitality. O'Malley's Emporium, am I right? Hospitality. 'Cause so far, my review is all suck."

"What?" I said. Both the robot and I looked to him.

The robot began to fold itself up, in front of our eyes, like for storage or transport. Marmite cast a glance at me. One interpretation would be that it wilted under Marmite's stern demands, except that outside in the salvage yard, all the robots were doing the same. Folding, hunkering down.

That was when we were hit by our first gravity wave. Of course you don't know what it is, so suddenly you're ill, you're fainting. I swooned.

"Artificial gravity wave," Marmite said, bracing himself upright, boots flat on the floor but otherwise unfazed.

"What? What? That's a thing?"

"No, but it's theoretically possible. If the planet has a floating metal core of variable density."

Marmite was a man with two brains. He had his normal moron brain, but also... "It sure dropped the birds," I said, quietly. One minute there were sooty sparrows flitting around the yard, then the gravity wave brought them down. It was a funny sight, really. One minute, it's sing, sing... like all birds, they think they're the man. Then wham, down like stone. On the ground they were just little dust balls. "Marmite, look at that nose art, going up the conveyer belt? You recognise it?"

Marmite wasn't much interested. "A dinner fork?"

The gravity stopped, and our robot unfolded itself fastidiously.

The pieces on the conveyer belt were from our fleet. "It's the *Bonhomme Richard*. Is this place off the charts or something? How many ships augured-in?"

Marmite ignored me and returned to our robot companion. "So, girls and drinks."

"Girls?" I said. "Girls? Scan the perimeter, man. I'd say no girls in this time zone."

"Keep cool, Milo," Marmite wore an expression of secret, superior knowledge. "O'Malley's Emporium. It's what this place is famous for." To the robot, he called, "Tell my man O'Malley that I want to see him."

The robot had its own confusions. "What is this... seventh?"

Finally. This was a new voice. Instead of a programmed robot, this was a man talking. We didn't know who it was or where it was from, but it was definitely human, speaking through the robot by radio.

"Are you being serious with me? You're not being serious with me," Marmite answered the voice. "You haven't heard of the Seventh?"

"The Seventh Armored Cavalry," I said, losing patience. "*Ut in Fumum.*"

"There he is," Marmite said. "Love the beard, man, now..."

A man watched us from the yard, through the window, little fat guy in homespun, one of O'Malley's thousand great-grandsons. His walkie-talkie was half static... "...our founding fathers ... our foundational rights to neutrality ... founding fathers..."

"Yeah," said Marmite, riding over the broken message. "We're not so much interested in visiting the statues, this trip. We'll save the museums, keep that in reserve, another time. Just get us a phone. Our ship crashed. We're space ambassadors, first class."

"Founding fathers..."

One difficulty on that crap planet was communication. Because of their gravity games, the planet had no satellites. Add to this, the inhabitants could never get it together enough to lay cables. It was a problem of property rights.

Our guy became agitated, looming over his handset until he could shout straight down into it. It was an ancient walkie-talkie with an extendible chrome antenna that waved around almost a metre. To end the discussion, dramatically, he tried to push the antenna back inside the case with one single motion. Instead it bent sideways, and his emotional finish was lost in static.

Bang! Ominously, shutters began to lower over the window. The robot squeaked, and returned to its old recorded voice. "By stepping foot on a private world, you have made the choice for liberty. This choice comes with obligations, however. The debt you have incurred..."

"Oh come on," I yelled. "Bring the other guy back."

"Liberty has never been free, and the most

important thing you own is your incurred obligations, for your needs do not entitle you to..."

Marmite stomped the hollow floor. "Are we really conversing with lawyer-pod? Hey! Beard-boy! Come back, tell us about how you found your father."

During this, our robot opened a hatch in its belly. It began counting out money, onto one of the empty seats between Marmite and me. It was weird local cash. Square bills, printed with numbers and designs. Foil coupons.

Marmite nodded at this sign of progress. "Are these our drink vouchers? Are these good anywhere? Or just certain consortiums?"

Its counting done, the robot slimmed itself and retreated through the door. The money lay where it had been dealt, in two piles. The shutters were down, and now the ceiling light dimmed. A promotional video began to play.

"Ah, come on, Law Spider!" Marmite called after. "Can we skip the briefing? Aw. At least get some beers in here? Put these cupholders to purpose?"

No response, and with the video running, Marmite immediately fell asleep. So I got to learn alone.

No surprises, really. I'd already figured most of it. O'Malley's Emporium was one of these "free-trade" planets. There were dozens of these things, scattered across the galaxy. On these places there were no rights or anything like that, except property rights. Before you landed you had to agree to all their rules in advance. Basically the founding principle was that you got to keep your stuff. What the dudes feared most was having to subsidize school lunch.

What can you say about these places? They were mostly harmless. A bit depressing, because they all looked like shit, and no women ever wanted to live there. There'd be these mournful wives or daughters, often fulfilling both roles, stuck with their bad cards

and their flimsy bonnets. Put a pall over the general
mood.

I had pretty much pegged the scene when I saw the
man's random beard. For some reason it was always
bearded dudes. They'd leave normal planets and
congregate. Each one would get a certain amount of
space that he could guard against intrusion.

The information video went on for hours. It served
the dual purpose of promotion and also informing us
of our incurred obligation, which we'd apparently
agreed to by crash-landing here.

When the video finished, the lights came back on.
"What was all that?" Marmite roused from where he
was passed out on in the aisle. "Law spider! I'm ready
to confess whatever, as long as you don't make us
watch that again." He called out, "Movie is done. Yo!
Show's over. I've been here for days. I've got to drain
the main vein."

He remembered the money and went to examine.
"Bigger stack is mine. So, give me the brief of the
brief."

"It's one of these freedom planets."

"Free love? Why don't they make bills that will fit a
man's wallet?"

"'We're lucky it's not raccoon furs."

"32,650." Marmite neatened his stack like a deck of
cards. "What's this minus sign?"

"It's debt dollars."

That was the cash system there. It worked in
reverse. To tell you the truth, I still don't get it. This
was O'Malley's private planet, and everyone owed him
something. The cash was our incurred obligation.
Instead of trying to acquire it, you tried to get rid of it.

Marmite raged and carried on until I cut him off:
"Listen! Did you hear an explosion?"

He wouldn't shut up, he was so mad about the reverse money.

"I'm not going to justify the place, the whole time we're down here, just because I couldn't sleep during the lecture. Listen. Something is going on."

The shutter began to peel back. Someone was wrecking it by peeling back the metal with a crowbar. I saw a face.

"Some kind of animal?" Marmite said, testing his cuffs. He'd gotten his foot up in there.

"Not an animal."

"What was it, like a Tony? A baby Tony?"

"It was the most beautiful girl in the world."

"What? Oh. Right. Finally. Did I see? Was she wearing an eye patch?"

5.

The fox ladies didn't have a name for themselves as a separate species. They were probably christened something by the humans that created them. In fact, later on I did hear some slang terms, pretty vile, but nothing for use, and maybe forgotten now, lost in history.

From the moment the fox ladies broke into the room, you could tell that Marmite and I were an unhappy surprise to them. They were all young women, which was odd but some militaries are like that. And of course Marmite and I were big, smelly men. The fox ladies had discovered the groggy marine ladies in our crashed ship, counted hibernation pods, and figured we were two more women marines, captured by O'Malley's robots.

So – they made it no secret – our rescuers were disappointed. What I didn't know was that we almost got the spike right then. Some voted to pin us to our seats, let us bleed out on the industrial carpet.

What saved us was the debt money, carpeting the place. Marmite was enraged to learn he hadn't been issued casino vouchers. He ripped and tore them and threw them around the room. The fox ladies hated that debt money almost as much as they hated men, and they were kind of impressed by the sincerity of Marmite's violence.

We were uncuffed and led away into the scruffy forest, but the spirit of joyous rescue was lacking. For one, the bearded guy with the walkie-talkie was out there dead, lying under a tractor. A number of his joints had been broken, for his shoulders to splay out the way they did, and he had quantities of the foil money in his mouth. Believe me, if he died choking on that worthless tinfoil, that was better than the other damage he showed, which included removal of his man parts.

I was sobered by these events, and by what was getting to be a pretty full duty day, but more than that I was stunned by the beauty of the woman who led the rescue. Mildred. Like a lot of beautiful women, she stole all colour and light from the world around her, leaving her sister companions dull and matronly. Only she had ever moved with such grace.

She was the entire rebellion. She was the centre of it. The fox ladies were bred to be docile, or at most playfully naughty. For their sick legal purposes, the scientists had to dilute the human blood by 1/8. Most of the changes were to the useless tail of the DNA, but being sick pudges, and not particularly imaginative, the science boys thought of foxes, and they altered some superficial aspects of appearance. (Even Marmite called them the "foxy ladies" for a time.)

But with Mildred, some fool scientist flipped his

chart upside down. He swapped his test tubes. The animal part of Mildred wasn't for looks. It was fucking real. They bred a cannibal commando.

Also, she could pass her verve to the others. Her followers didn't crowd her, but they moved in relation to her. They watched her even when they weren't watching her. She was their *leader*.

It was the first time I'd ever seen one. I didn't even know a leader was a real thing. In the military, "leader" and "leadership" are standard cue words that whatever is being said is bullshit. (Not that cue words are super necessary.) The particular meaning of "leadership" is that you're just supposed to do whatever. You're not supposed to ask how come it's a stupid idea. But I guess the concept was a real one, and derived from what I saw with Mildred.

In the fight for the salvage station, a robot had sliced Mildred across her belly. She didn't care about a little thing like blood leaking down over her thighs, but when we stopped in the shade of some pines, one of her sisters sprayed sealant on the wound. "No, no," I said. "Wait between coats. Just a second." The sister didn't know to hold the can upright. I took it and showed her. I put on a coat. I blew to dry where it puddled.

"Doesn't work on me," Mildred growled to the world. "I'm not human."

I looked up. My medical care had attracted a party of fox ladies. They were puzzled, tittering but not nicely. Their mean smiles showed sharp teeth, pretty far back in the mouth.

The scene held the whiff of danger. One aspect I certainly hadn't considered: when I knelt to blow on Mildred's skin, my face was right there, my face was warmed by the steam of her midriff. And now my pants were going to explode, because my dick grew three sizes, like the Grinch's heart. Turned on? Yes, like a tidal wave hitting a sand castle. Mildred's scent and shape blew every valve at once, and there was no longer any control over the flow of fluids. I didn't dare look down. My pants creaked ominously, like a gas tank in a bonfire.

Mildred champed her teeth and called out, "Did we take the guts from the corpse?"

Her followers chattered and self-abased, at having disappointed.

"No better snack." With her mouth she pretended to suck a strand of spaghetti, swallowing in gulps to accommodate for the twists of an intestine.

The stupidest fox ladies started back to the salvage depot. At this point it would be crawling with military robots, but they were going to go anyway. I guess they were all pretty stupid because I could see that Mildred's whole thing was an act, a pretty transparent act. She overdid it, what a monster she was. Anyone could see the beautiful girl inside her.

"Let me get your elbow," I said, still holding the can of sealant. "You've got a hole there."

That got more titters. "Here's the hole they put in me." Mildred raised her eye patch to show the empty socket. She did it for effect, like she was a carnival exhibit. I looked away, and she barked with sick triumph. "It was no crime to discipline a pet."

Look, there's no reason to dwell on it. In the constitution O'Malley had drawn up, he put in usual language about human slavery. You have to put something like that in or the Intergalactic Court doesn't let you claim a planet. Okay, good enough. But O'Malley went ahead and defined the term "human". Then to answer his glaring need for women, his scientists created these ladies that were only 7/8 humans. These they could make and buy and sell.

Genetic engineering is expensive. The created ladies

began life with a lot of debt. Mildred still carried a satchel of her foil certificates around and, believe me, you did not want to receive one.

What can you say about O'Malley? Obviously this "rights" business poisons your brain. You declare rights to this and that, even if it's nuts, like suddenly one man has a right to all the food. Gets it together in a pile, and sits on it like a dragon. If he has the legal paperwork, he starts to think it's okay. He's even got the word confusion: it's "right".

Indulge these fantasies, and it wasn't long before O'Malley felt that he had the right to everything. The little girls he made, and everything in the sky. Every space ship that wandered in to take a look. In the spirit of an earth law about territorial waters, or old explorers claiming a river and all its drainage valley, so too had O'Malley claimed anything feathered by the touch of his planet's gravity.

All right. So Marmite and I had landed ourselves in the midst of a civil war. No – wrong – that overstates it. O'Malley was in charge. He had a perfectly good mech force. He lived on an island that floated in quicksilver and somehow shielded him from the worst of the gravity excesses. This place was comically fortified, completely unassailable, and Mildred didn't even think about attacking with her ragtag band. She and her former slaves (or "debtors") occasionally roughed up O'Malley's salvage robots. That was about all they were capable of.

Recently the rebels had been augmented by parties of castaways. When we got to the main camp, there were some shell-shocked merchant crews wandering around (though only women). With all the war activity in the last year, O'Malley had pulled down so many spaceships that he hadn't been able to collect all the new debt hostages.

As Mildred and I talked, she stopped me dead with a description of some of the new arrivals, who were aliens.

"Frogs? You've got a Frog camp?"

"They're useless." She dismissed anyone who couldn't assist her raids.

"Frogs? Sure, they're mostly blow, but some of them are deadly. Are we talking about the same thing? Little guys? Yeah? Arrogant? Are there any with fins on their heads?"

She shrugged. "They play a drum." To her, that said it all about their uselessness.

"How about Tonies?" I asked carefully, "Any of those around?" We had our first argument because Mildred liked the sound of these Tony characters. I tried to convince and she swooned over each bloody detail. Because of her grim life experience, she mistook all aliens for her natural allies, anything that had a track record for killing human men.

I began to imagine Tonies leaping out of the trees. "The marines are okay? You brought their weapons out of the wreckage, didn't you? "

"They're not talking."

"They're marines. I don't think they ever really talk much." Mildred examined my statement. "I'm kidding around. They've still got drugs in them. The ship doses you so it can land."

I explained our situation. Space war. Ambassador mission. She explained hers. Rebellion against sicko O'Malley. The sun began to go down, and Mildred went to check the camp pickets.

"Bro, you don't have to take the one with the broken face."

"What?"

Marmite hurried by, in high colour. "Bro, there are dozens of prime! Did I tell you, or did I tell you? 'A man does not go unlaid on O'Malley's Emporium.'"

"What?"

"Something is wrong. Something is slipping. It is your fault. Is it your fault?" Alone in the dim of her command tent, Mildred quit pretending that her mouth had trouble with language. Her visit to the pickets had been unsatisfactory. "They're not... hungry. They're so lazy, lately. It's as though they've given up." She struggled to find the words, and that struggle became part of it. "It's like a fog."

I held her.

"Let me go," she said. She stepped back and showed teeth, ratcheting them over one another, *ting ting ting*, like the tines of a couple of forks. This elongated her face and showed she was an animal. "Soldier, do you think that you are seducing me?"

"Oh fuck off," I said. "This is Milo here. Burper Team One. Call in your crew, if you want an audience for your stupid vampire act. Vampire princess."

I didn't go away. She didn't go away. For apology, she said, "You know they *did* a fox hunt, once, with one of my sisters. They had horses and horns and dogs. They had to create the horses first."

We stood there looking at each other for a time. She said, "It's not real. I was designed to allure."

"What dipshit told you that? 'Designed.' You can't listen to dipshits, it encourages them, they proliferate."

She smiled a human smile, but it was sad. Her mind went back to her inadequate forces. "They will crush us out. We were six hundred, when we broke free."

Six hundred? From what I'd seen, Mildred had only about seventy ladies remaining. I had no idea it was such total war.

Clearly what Mildred needed to do was escape. She needed to stop attacking, hunker down, and get her sisters off the crap planet. But what could I offer? I didn't have a ship or a plan. "They can't touch you out here. No robot can tangle with a space marine."

She tuned her sad smile. "Your marines won't fight. Your mission was to negotiate with O'Malley."

"I guess that was the original purpose. The fleet needs this place for staging and supplies. There are plans to invade several planets out this way. They're invading one of them now."

I thought of my mates in the Seventh Cavalry, landing on Mikel, the Tony homeworld. At that moment, I imagined that my thoughts were with them, riding into battle. I probably even gazed at the ceiling of the tent. But of course there was no real battle, just a massacre as they landed, and I was just waxing sentimental, and my mates were all dead.

Mildred said, "We won't be important to this contract."

What she said had an uncomfortable ring of truth. If the fleet wanted O'Malley's Emporium as a port, we would put up with a lot. "You're not far wrong," I admitted.

"He'll know how to wring every advantage from your people."

"O'Malley?"

"I know him." She touched her face. I'm not big on vengeance and grudges and all that, but if I met this O'Malley, I would sure kick his ass for him, free of charge.

"Let me kiss you," I said.

It was a mistake. She gasped a little, and turned away, genuinely upset. She mumbled something and was out the tent flap. She was crying.

When I looked out on the camp, she had disappeared. She was nowhere to be seen. It was a shoddy camp, with improvised tarp tents. Everything was made with rubber ropes to account for the variable gravity.

Looking at the jumble, my earlier idea took shape. We could just load the ladies on a transport, relocate them to a planet that wasn't owned by a greedy shitbag.

"You getting it in? It's beer slow for me, I admit, slow, but plans are set now. Horizontal groove. I think I plans with this one who's..."

"Marmite?" There he was, trying to look pleased but mostly confused. He jabbered. As usual, because I'd been talking to someone normal, it took a long moment to begin to understand Marmite's word patterns. As I made the necessary mental adjustment, a cold hand settled over my heart. "Wait. That was the term you used, 'horizontal groove.'"

Marmite talked on.

"But you used that specific term," I said. "Okay. Maybe. Dumbfuck, these ladies were brothel slaves. Don't proposition them like a drunken sailor. What are you thinking? Where the fuck do you think we are? Did you see the bearded dude back at the trailer?"

"Santa Claus? I figured he ran off. Woo-hoo! He high-tailed it..."

"Ran off? Is your head up your ass?" Actually, at the moment, it was a relief to remember that Marmite *did* have his head up his ass. "You're sure you called it 'horizontal groove'? Thank god for that. Thank god. You just said your usual things?"

"Milo?"

We'd been saved by this before. Marmite's pickup lines were incomprehensible. Most girls didn't know what he was talking about. They thought he was a simpleton, with a private language of his own, or a foreign-exchange student. They listened with polite curiosity, pleasant expression, trying their best, mild furrowing of the brows. When he finished, they'd pantomime directions to the toilet.

"Milo?"

"Marmite, she didn't understand you. Thank god."

Marmite agreed there were translation difficulties, and explained.

"No, 'patriarchy' is a real word," I muttered.

"I couldn't... so I showed her the paper."

I stopped him. "Paper?"

Even Marmite had begun to sense something was wrong, after his long, frustrating afternoon. Now, to avoid my blame and reprimand, he adopted the escape strategy of a bunny rabbit, which was to become completely still and expressionless.

"What's on the paper, Marmite? Marmite." I smacked his face with open palm.

"I got one for you, man! I got tons of them. I took the whole stack."

"Show me the paper, Marmite."

With sighs and reluctance, Marmite got a wad from his pocket. They were glossy fliers. They advertised a brothel. The catch-phrase was, "A man does not go unlaid on O'Malley's Emporium."

The brochure folded out. On the front, the fox ladies were dressed in bangles and can-can dresses. Inside the photos were explicit. There were explicit pricelists. "All whims accommodated."

"Marmite..." My voice was stunned to a whisper. "Marmite, Marmite..."

How did I know what was coming? I had the brochure unfolded, and now I flipped it. The entire back was one explicit poster. I recognised the girl, though this was before she had lost an eye. "Holy shit."

"Yeah, that's what I..."

"You gave one of these...?" I confirmed. I scanned the camp. No signs of uproar. "Okay, most of them can't read. Okay..."

A harsh public voice cut through. "'The bearer of this is entitled to one free screw.'" It was Mildred. Mildred read with no difficulty. She had a very tall fox lady next to her, blonde and confused, Marmite's counterpart. More ladies gathered from the shadows. "A screw? With all the metal parts, broken in our dirt, we can give you better than that..."

She held the paper. Her sturdy nails worked to rip the coupon from the rest.

All right, don't judge Mildred for jumping to conclusions. Consider from her perspective. To her, our real purpose for landing on O'Malley's Emporium was to taste the pleasures of its bawdy houses.

"Do not kill... these ones," she told her party, her voice labouring over the words. She wore a new eye patch, or with the evening sun I could see the pattern of hair follicles for the first time. It was a human scrotum, leatherized. A long, curved spike grew out of her elbow.

"Marmite," I said. "Run."

6.

The Pit of Woe had been so-named in some earlier date. No one down there was unhappy except me.

The Pit of Woe was the prison pit for all men, the space crews who had been marooned by O'Malley's gravity trick and been captured by the fox ladies instead of O'Malley's robot force.

The Pit was a giant natural earth cave, sometimes crudely braced but mostly not, so that the only ceiling was the fine hair of tree roots. Marmite and I had not been there a minute when a three G gravity wave rolled over the planet and brought down a rain of soil. All signs pointed to us being buried alive, but there was no panic. The other prisoners were dozens of men, sitting calmly in a circle. None of them cared much.

I didn't fucking care, I wanted to drown in dirt.

"Good morrow, friend," one of the men greeted me. He turned to Marmite, "Good morrow, friend."

"Eh?" I thought my back was broke. The Pit of Woe was a prison in the spirit of those prisons where you're put to die of starvation and neglect, out of sight. Your term of incarceration started with you being thrown down a ten-metre hole, which should have meant that we were all dead in a pile with broken necks, but you bounced off the irregular walls coming down, and the inmates had piled straw.

"I wished you good morrow."

"Oh, all right." My first look was dozens of men sitting cross-legged, in a calm circle. They were a strange crew, these fellows, emaciated but happy, even playful. The cave went off for kilometres in some directions, but mostly everyone hung out there around the crash-pad, the only spot with sun.

I wasn't happy company. I dragged off to the edge and spent a few days staring into the darkness, remembering the expression on Mildred's face, which was a mix of fury and a broken heart. Like I took a toy from an orphan. It killed me. Anything else, I could have taken. She could have given me the spike. That would have killed me too, but this killed me worse. Mildred held the brochure, looking from it to me, back again. I'll never forget.

I brooded, and the weird skeletal gents left me alone. Except for Marmite who kept bugging me.

"Bro, an easy escape. A gimmee." He shook his head. "These guys don't have a plan. They don't plan anything." After a moment he tried again. "I been counting guards. I don't even think they guard the drop tunnel. Sometimes, when they throw stuff down."

He was hurt that I ignored him, but this seemed fair, seeing that he cost me the love of my life.

"There's a Tony here," he said. "Got thrown down like an hour before us. Yeah. Milo? Aren't you going to puke or something?"

"I assume it's dead, if it's not killing us."

"It's alive. It's fine, I think. It's stunned or something."

"He contemplates on the Love Prince." This was one of the veteran prisoners. When they did talk, they would say things like that.

One surprise, when I got hungry, there was plenty of food. Apparently it wasn't always like this, but lately there was plenty. Stuff would come raining down, until there was a pile to one side that spilled like a cornucopia. The prisoners would snack, but no one seemed too interested.

The more I paid attention to the prison atmosphere, the less I understood. We got visited by the space marines. Pembroke, Manfred, and Geppetto. They visited, called down from the rim, tossed flowers they'd gathered.

"Some kind of sick mockery?" I asked.

Marmite waved back to the three. During my time brooding, they had established communication. "I think it's kind of nice."

"They're blowing kisses," I said. Marmite offered no explanation, and indeed, there was none that could be offered. These were marine ladies, square-jawed, salted, seventy-years-old. They chewed tobacco and all three would turn and spit at once, synchronized by long habit. Back on the space ship they scared the shit out of me, with their knife games, but now they were lovey-dovey.

"Robots down here, too," Marmite said, still waving the flower he caught. "I wonder why they throw those down."

"I'm not sure you've picked up on this. The fox ladies aren't all super smart. These are salvage robots?"

Marmite brought me to an inner chamber, where a card game was dimly lit by a robot's chest plate. Most of the robot's limbs were busted but the power plant obviously worked, if the stick men were using the light. "Turn on the brain, not the body," I said.

"I know what I'm doing, man. You're going talk with it?"

I ignored him and whistled a few stevedore notes over and over, basically "keep calm, keep calm". The robot chest was a crude screen. My skills aren't A1, but after some monkeying I got a rough map of salvage sites. The chart was useless to me, just kilograms of metal harvested.

Marmite waited like a puppy to be helpful. "All right," I huffed. "You try. The ships they've downed. Do they have them by name?"

Of course for Marmite the robot immediately spat data. "Some of them, some of them..."

"*Bonhomme Richard*. No. No. I'll spell it... It's a naval freighter. Carried ammunition to Helicon 7."

"Milo, could there be a Burper?"

"Would you say that's likely?" I snapped. "Based on all the luck I've enjoyed?" The robot couldn't do names but did have visuals of crash sites. It shuffled through them. "Shit, stop," I said. I scanned for minute. Checked the time stamp. Scanned again.

The card players had never stopped their lazy game. I couldn't understand the rules. They took turns drawing, or handing each other cards, and always said "thank you", so it wasn't clear if they wanted to hold more or less. With no other recourse, I placed my hand over the deck. "All right, gents." I rubbed my face. "Tell me about the Love Prince."

Frog ships were easy to identify, because they were built to look like the Frogs themselves. This Frog ship crashed nine months earlier. Point of origin? Helicon 7. Crashed intact. Debtors presumed but not recovered.

From there, events were easy to piece together. Back

on Helicon 7, the superfrogs visited Marmite's brain. They survived the experience but had their own minds blown, or written over, permanently fried. Survivors somehow made it here, at least one of them. He called himself the Love Prince, and, from what I could see, he was sending out waves of mellow.

Once you thought of it in those terms, all was explained. These prison boys behaved as though they'd smoked a bong-load. Mildred's blood-thirsty crew would rather nap and giggle than pursue vengeance. Even Mildred – she declined to crucify me and Marmite, though she had motive and opportunity.

The powers of the Love Prince extended to every living creature. The trees and bushes and grass quit competing for space. They shared and took turns. "Oh man." I knelt and studied the ants on the ground. Yes, the black ants were giving the red ants piggyback rides. It was unbelievable.

And in one of the side chambers, the Tony castaway lay comatose. It lay there, blank-eyed, day and night. Tonies had only venom inside. With that gone, I'm surprised the thing kept breathing.

"Oh, poor girl," I muttered quietly. Mildred was trying to hold together her rebellion while her troops were high as a kite. Her foes, at least the robots, wouldn't be slowed by whatever messages the Love Prince was sending out.

Probably if I told Mildred what I knew, she would seek out this Love Prince character and kill him. Stuff his carcass into his drum. Up to this point she had ignored the Frog encampment because they were harmless, useless, and, as far as anyone could tell, not men.

Now, I had no love for Frogs. I had killed maybe a hundred thousand, and by and large they were cruel little squish toys. But the Love Prince didn't seem to me the prime hitch in this situation.

"There you be," Marmite said.

I looked up from the ants. On the robot's chest was a picture of the *Bonhomme Richard*. The tail of the ship was crushed. Most of the cargo area seemed okay. I didn't ask, but while I watched Marmite somehow called up the cargo manifest.

"Right. That's my luck," I said. "Pattern intact." The *Bonhomme Richard* was hauling war materiel. Good! It was hauling armoured vehicles. Good! It was hauling SPUMes.

Back out in the main chamber, the Marine ladies called down, "Yoo-hoo! Yoo-hoo!"

Marmite wanted to stay and be helpful to me. But he also wanted to go and play. "Go ahead," I said. "But, hey, tell them to throw down a rope."

The SPUMe vehicle was a burrowing craft, based on captured Frog technology. (Frog vehicles often burrowed.) The SPUMe was unbelievably slow, and dangerous only to its driver or anyone who relied upon it to accomplish a mission. When it had proven useless for combat, it was repurposed to reconnaissance, where its uselessness was just as glaring but more difficult to document.

A SPUMe didn't drill a tunnel or anything like that. It didn't actually dig. It used an enormous, leaky powerplant to move the ground particles in front of the vehicle to behind the vehicle. You just needed a bubble to start. That's your picture: Think of navigating a bubble through the mucky bowels of a planet. The steering was thrown together with rubberbands.

I had about finished preparations for launch when a voice froze me. "Pretty." Mildred touched the nose cone, and was baffled by the supple skin, as well she might be. It was like calf hide. "What is it called?"

"This thing? Um. Yeah, I'm not sure. It hasn't so

much been named, I think. It's a light vehicle. For spying, I think, so not heavily armed." I talked at random. Mildred was alone, and she didn't move to kill me. "In fact no guns," I said. "In fact I don't know why it exists."

"Can you navigate it?"

"You mean, can I drive it?" I took a full breath, in and out. "Look, I know I've got no high ground with you, but that question... How many times do I have to tell people, I drive the Burper, the Big fucking Burper, the most prodigious fighting vehicle known to man, and the mainstay of the Seventh Cavalry. Thirty-six gears. What about that isn't clear?"

"Okay, okay." This Mildred was calm, or worn out. Her whole life had been a fight.

During my rant, I had pulled out my lapel to show the Seventh Cavalry insignia. But I forgot I wasn't wearing my uniform. "Yeah, ambassador duds," I explained. It was not a great look, short tunic for a short lady.

"Don't walk over any air grates," Mildred said. She gave me a slow, flirtatious smile. "You've got twenty centimetres of leeway. Don't walk over any mirrors."

She gave me ten minutes of chat. Every minute I fell in love again, if I hadn't been in full love already. Most of her life Mildred was a professional girl, and when I tried to get heavy she had ways to deflect me. I would start to profess, and she would tease me back in line.

I think she enjoyed it too. She played with the idea of coming along. She thought it was suicide but it would also be like the Tunnel of Love. The two of us would bubble along down there in the dark.

She shook off the vision. For all her playfulness, she knew the facts. If she was gone, pretty soon all her sisters would be dead. She said, "You won't make it. I know you're a decorated soldier... am I allowed to tell you that his island is a fortress?"

"Oh, I mean, a fortress as concept is pretty much obsolete. There *is* an element of science experiment, apparently, when I hit the lake of pure mercury. Apparently the island floats in a moat of mercury, like adjustable pilings of mercury, and Marmite says there's a chance the burrow drive might ignite it. But he didn't seem too concerned." Truth to tell, Marmite wasn't too concerned about anything when I left him. He sat behind his Marine fiancée, trying to braid flowers into her coarse bristles of her grey hair.

I couldn't have taken Mildred anyway, even if she insisted. The worthless SPUMe frame only carried 400 kilograms. So, 100 for me, and 300-plus for a huge piece of comatose cargo.

How's that as an atmosphere for a first kiss? Impending death. Apparently Mildred had never kissed before, and I had never kissed anyone with the carnivore mouth configuration. Meanwhile, within easy reach, so close I can smell it, we have your Tony, bound, wrapped, cuffed, and asleep in the back seat.

I drove all night. Once out of range of the Love Prince's influence, the Tony began to rouse, and it was this groggy but reviving Tony I dropped off in O'Malley's private quarters. The SPUMe could surface right through the rock foundation, and right through the marble floors. The rooms were deserted. All the walls were big-screen televisions.

I suppose the Tony roamed there and desecrated until O'Malley came home from the office. What happened next? O'Malley got to meet his first Tony, and the Tony race got to meet their first hero of property rights. How did they greet each other? Of what did they speak? Records are scant. Evidence is scant. Some colour on the floor of the foyer.

But before O'Malley went home to that surprise, he met with me, in my role of ambassador (somewhat overstated). We hammered out some deals, he and I. Some contracts. O'Malley was pretty concerned about his financial liability. On the table between us was the bent licence plate Marmite had twisted off the salvage bot. Whenever O'Malley asserted the strength of his position, I could point out spots of blood of the Marine gal.

O'Malley. Brother. I'll spare you the details. I already told you he was an asshole, and you're just going to have to trust me. Normally I couldn't have stayed ten minutes in that room. What helped was that I knew he had the Tony waiting. I had to keep that vision in mind, and we negotiated.

However – I'll tie it up – the episode ended pretty badly. As I'd come to expect, when I finally got in touch with the fleet, I was buried with complaints about the contracts I'd signed with O'Malley. I'd done it all wrong. Sure, the fleet could land and resupply, but no one could make heads or tails of the idea of debt money (not my fault), or how ownership rights for an entire continent could be transferred to an entity known simply as "Love Frog".

This barrage of complaint was interrupted with a notice that I had been promoted to Brigadier General. What? I had to read to paragraph eight before it became clear that the promotion was not a reward for competence and heroism but instead a computer-generated move. It happened automatically. The command rank passed because I was the foremost surviving member. Except for Marmite and me, everyone in the Seventh Cavalry was dead.

That was the only reference to the massacre I ever encountered, but it was clear enough. I read it again. The Seventh Cavalry was gone. The Seventh.

And after that, what is there to say?

Nebuchadnezzar

Michael B. Tager

We're stopped somewhere in the middle of the great plain, between the barely developed archipelagos – with the spaceport and grand Cathedral – and the slightly-more developed, rich in metal deposits, west coast. The maps in the manual are very detailed, but even so, we're in the middle of nowhere. Mountains far in the distance to the north and east wink at us, obscured by mist and scattered scrub-trees. Normally, we keep to a schedule of travel; awake at dawn, travel through lunch, break down three hours before sundown. But today, a herd of buffalo pass us, taking their time. The herd numbers thousands and I know that this is what it must have been like back on Earth, before they were all wiped out.

The soldiers confer with Hans, our leader, and agree that we should all stop. We've been advised to keep our distance from the soldiers, the leader especially. The scuttlebutt is they were conscripted upon arrival due to "unsavoury concerns". I've parsed this as: they were unwilling colonists with criminal histories. Are the soldiers protecting us or herding us? Two of the biggest soldiers – one tall and lanky, the other broad and scarred – look like sheep hounds when at ease.

We circle up, our wagons staring at each other, and pitch camp, stow our gear. It's when I'm done that one of the astras comes close to the tent I share with Andre, a fat French teenager who actually petitioned his parents and parish to be sent along with the rest of our two hundred colonists. He ignores the astra, except to kick purple dirt at it from time to time and mutter French curses he thinks I don't understand.

"Come here, Hagar," I say to the creature. Its floppy, membranous ears twitch at the sound, but it doesn't respond. In no way have the astras acclimated to our presence on their planet. Colonists only touched down – in planetary terms – half a second ago. It's a good thing for them we don't find them edible, or they'd likely be extinct by now.

According to our "Welcome to Eden" manuals, the astradents normally come out only at night. They have one large tooth, a prehensile tail and four small, humanlike hands. The initial surveys indicated rudimentary life forms, like Earth a hundred million years before the dinosaurs. The seed ships and terraformers dumped millions of tons of water and oxygen, and then the life of Earth, from microbes up to echidnas, onto TSX-59 to turn it into Eden. After all that almost all the native life had died. The manual doesn't really explain much beyond that.

I wait for it to respond. When it doesn't, I toss my bread crust and watch it disappear into the astra's mouth and into the lengthening shadows. Eden has longer (twenty-six hours) and hotter (sixty-five degrees versus sixty-one) days than Earth, but only barely and I've become accustomed to it after six weeks.

"You shouldn't feed those things," Andre says. He sits next to me and claps my shoulder with a meaty, freckled hand. "They are pests. You would not feed rats, no?" I don't respond and after a moment he heaves himself to his feet and sighs. "You are still thinking of your sisters, yes? Your family?"

"Yes." My voice breaks; I know they died hundreds of years ago, but for me, it's only been a few months. Andre winces and hangs his head, mumbling prayer intended for my soul. *What an unfortunate time*, I think. Yes, I am sad, but I am also fifteen. Voices break.

He thinks over his next words and says, "I am going to the chaplain. I will pray for you." For a big boy, his feet are surprisingly light and I barely hear him walk away into the heart of the camp. Hans – an amiable Nigerian priest – is the only ordained adult in our group and wears many hats: chaplain, navigator, cook. He's offered me his time before, but he's so busy, I'd feel guilty taking his help.

While I sit on the Navy-surplus stool in front of my Navy-surplus tent, waiting for the alien heat to vanish and the alien night to come on, I feel very sorry for myself. It is only after I let a sob escape my throat that I hear the chuckling from behind me.

I whirl, falling off the stool, and set the girl to laughing. I lie on the ground, stunned, while she stubs out her cigarette and approaches me, extending her hand. "You ok?" she asks, helping me to my feet.

"I'm fine." I brush the purple dirt off my white muslin missionary clothes.

"That's good," she says. She's short, barely comes to my chest, with big green eyes, curly brown hair, pale skin, fat cheeks. She smells of cigarettes and... I lean closer...

"You've been drinking," I say, unable to keep the reproach out of my tone. I am shocked, but more, I'm surprised. *Where did she get that?*

The girl purses her lips and grumbles deep in her throat. I'm used to that from disapproving Sunday school teachers, not from girls my age. "It's really none of your concern, Joseph," she says, "but this is the first time I've ever had anything to drink at all. The soldiers," she motions to the adjoining camp where the masked militia escorting us spends their off-time, "have access to all kinds of things." She sniffs and tosses her hair back from where it's fallen across her eyes. For a second she seemed far older than her years; now she looks younger than me. I wonder how she knows my name, but she continues, "I think I'll be going."

She swivels, her muslin shift barely moving (her hem is coated in a thin layer of purple dust, barely visible in the dim light). While she walks away, I remember how all of our clothes were taken away from us after we'd awoke from cryo, ice still clinging to our eyebrows and our cheeks, light-years of sleep still heavy on us. My fingers were barely functioning when they removed my duffel bag full of my meagre possessions. Heavy-set men in solemn robes took my things, mouthed platitudes about being free from sin that I couldn't understand; all I understood was that they were being burned, that we'd receive the acceptable leftovers later. I'm still waiting; I know Andre is too.

Within moments, the girl disappears into the shadows and the night is upon me. I retake my seat on the surplus-stool and watch the darkness. After a little while, I crawl into the little tent and fall asleep.

It's another week before I see her again. Of course, I *see* her around between meetings; there are only one hundred of us pilgrims along with half-dozen chaperones, the chaplain and the nearly-invisible contingent of soldiers; the rest of the colonists stayed near the spaceport. I'm unclear on why the soldiers are with us. Are they there to kill the astradents? Is there a seditious army of infidel-Jewslims? Courtesy of the manual: "the population of Eden is just under one hundred thousand souls, spread out over a landmass roughly twice the size of Eurasia."

During orientation, we were given a brief rundown of what TSX-59 was like now that it had been redubbed Eden. New Jerusalem and the surrounding area contained eighty percent of the population and all the government. The spaceport and archipelago have the scientists and rudimentary manufacturing; it's petroleum heavy and where all the diesel comes from. Only five per cent of the world's population lives anywhere besides those two locales: independent men and women, all Christian of course, who struck out on their own, educate their own children, raise their own livestock and interact only to trade goods.

It sounds kind of nice to me. I want to ask someone what they think, but I can't think of who. No one seems interested. And I don't know anyone besides Andre and now, maybe, this girl. Regardless, we don't speak again for a week. Our group is highly segregated while we travel to New Jerusalem; the sects mingle some, though none integrate well with the Catholics. I travel with the Mennonites though I'm actually Quaker. I'm the only one in this group and they're the largest group – but the boys and girls are kept very separate, even within our sects. Only during prayers and meals do we see each other, and often meals are twenty minute breaks in the middle of a dust blown prairie, the eerie purple sky of TSX-59 above us. The water is purple, the dirt is purple, the sky is purple. Someone told me it had something to do with the methane content of the atmosphere being higher than Earth's, but I'm not sure I believe it.

The terraformers had less work to do here than any other planet humans have encountered since the advent of space exploration. I do believe that; why bother lying?

The astras follow our caravan. We move at a glacial pace, huge wooden wagon wheels carving new pathways in the dirt and the creatures can keep up with us without effort. My favourite astradent has come to know me and approaches me every night. I try to keep scraps of my meal to feed it, pieces of bread, scraps of meat. It isn't picky. It's while I'm feeding my friend – it's no longer Hagar, redubbed Ishmael – that the girl ambushes me again.

"Hi," she says, popping her head from behind the neighbouring tent and scaring little Ishmael to death. Its ugly eyes widen and it's gone in a puff of dust.

"Hey." This time I don't fall from my seat. For some reason, I'm glad that Andre is gone again to prayer. He's mentioned that I should be coming, that people are talking about me, that I'm not holy enough for them. But respectfully, as a friend should. As a good Christian should. He doesn't judge, he just worries. "You a Witness? I always see you with them."

She doesn't acknowledge the last bit, but sidles closer to me. In her palm she flashes a pack of cigarettes and raises her eyebrows. When I shake my head, she shrugs and sits in the dirt, her legs crossed. She palms a cigarette and lights it, takes a few quick drags and stubs it out. "My name's Helen," she says, offering her hand.

I shake it, surprised at how cool her palm is. "Joseph."

Helen giggles. "Of course it is. Seems like half the group is Joseph or Mary." She picks up a crust of bread on the ground and eyes the tiny bite marks, the indentations left by my little friend. "You like these things? The little alien-rats?"

"Technically, we're the aliens." Her lips twitch, like she wants to smile but doesn't quite know how it'll be taken. I continue. "But yeah, I like them. Admire them, a little."

"Why's that?" she asks. From somewhere in her robes, she produces a little black-and-gold journal, decorated with pencil drawings: skulls and unicorns.

I pause while she opens her journal, produces a pen from somewhere in her hair and starts sketching.

"They're survivors, I guess. They just do what they do, in this new world. They didn't choose to be here."

"Like me," Helen says, looking at me. "What about you? Did you choose to be here?"

I'm about to answer when I hear Andre singing, his surprisingly pleasant voice sounding nearer and nearer. The journal disappears and after a quick hug, so does Helen. Moments later, my friend returns.

"Ahh, you missed a good prayer meeting Joseph. There was much speaking in tongues." He sticks his hand into the tent and withdraws another little stool, flattened. He assembles it with practised snaps and sits, sighing and picking at something in his teeth. "This is a beautiful world for us. An entire empty land, ready for us to fill it with the word of Christ." He laughs and smacks me on the back. "Are you excited?"

After a moment, he moves the stool besides me and touches my shoulder. His eyes are dark pools of concerns. "Aren't you excited?"

New Jerusalem is on the peninsula that juts from the bottom of the west coast of Big Continent. On the map, it resembles a reverse Florida, even if the scale isn't quite right. Big Continent is just that... big, almost twice the size of North and South America put together. It's taken three months of travelling on our wagons and multiple service stops at little way-stations along the path to even get near New Jerusalem. Our wagons are diesel-powered and sturdy, but three months is a long time.

NJ was founded as the capital of TSX-59 in the region that most resembled biblical Eden. It's a lush area, where fig trees blossom and the natural bounty overwhelms. From there, the colonists spread out, a little more each year as the colony ships arrive and more and more babies are born. The birth rate, I've heard, is startling. Something like five babies born per woman.

Sometimes I count the women in our group. There are less than twenty in our group of one hundred, only Helen and half a dozen others of child-bearing age.

A month from our destination, we finally begin to see signs of civilization and we stop for a week at a little town named New Nazareth. Its similarity to its namesake stops there. A river flows next to it, brilliant purple water teeming with bass and catfish. Fishermen spend perhaps an hour throwing tossing lines and laughing before they go home, laden with food.

For miles around the town, crops grow to alarming sizes: corn ten feet tall, watermelons the size of small children. The weather here seems perfect for agriculture year round; it never gets too cold or too hot and rains one day out of five. It's a true paradise, for the astradents, too. I've only seen Francois (formerly Ishmael) once, outside the small window of the room I share with Andre. It sniffed at the ground beneath the window and whined. When I opened it, Francois reared up on hind legs and pawed at the air before dashing off.

We're staying at a hotel in the centre of town, a sprawling beast with dozens of dormitories, a saloon and three attached chapels. Andre and I, as the eldest of the male colonists, are given our own room just off the main dormitory where all the others snore. The girls are somewhere else; details are not given. When they're ferried off, I see one of the soldiers lean in close to Helen and whisper something. Her shoulder stiffens and she nods before the soldier ambles away.

For most of the first day, after we unpack our wagons, pray and eat, we sleep and read. From here to New Jerusalem, we'll be travelling in, hopefully, better style. The welcome packet included a map: towns and roads appear in greater numbers just past the river. I wish for trains and conveniences of Earth, but so far Eden lacks those resources. It's in the plans (according to the welcome packet) for a train system to be built "sometime" in the next fifty years.

I found a few discarded paperbacks in one of the lobbies and brought them back to my room. Most of them are typical trash that I throw aside, but two are exactly what I'm looking for: novels written with both style and panache without deviating from Christian morality. I read the sci-fi first, despite having travelled thousands of light years and hundreds of Earth-years to live on a planet with purple skies. My littlest sister is dead, buried and decomposed along with her children and her children's children, too. I don't like thinking about it.

Andre sniffs when he sees the book, but doesn't comment. He's on his bed in flannel pajamas, re-reading the Old Testament for the fifth time since we've arrived on TSX-59. The first few hours we heard the boys talking among themselves and laughing, but they soon fell asleep. Several peaceful hours later, I'm not surprised at all when the little window next to my bed slides up and Helen's head sticks through, followed by the rest of her. She reeks of beer. My oldest sister liked Milwaukee's Best and I remember the smell very well.

"The white masks," she says, her laugh bright and clear, "have strong beer if you know who to steal from." I haven't heard the soldiers called white masks before, but it makes sense. Their uniform is camouflage, but they wear half-masks that cover their mouth and chin.

"Merde!" Andre yells, jumping from the bed and spilling onto the floor.

I stifle my chuckle and tell him to be calm, that it's just a friend coming to say hello. When I open the window and help Helen through, Andre blushes and adjusts his pajama top. He begins to talk, but only stutters.

"It's ok, Andre," I say. "This is Helen."

He stands and sucks in his gut, scarlet still spread over his cheeks and neck. He nods at Helen, then extends a hand. "Nice to meet you," he says, his voice a squeak. He gives me a look – eyebrows bunched, teeth clenched – but keeps his voice calm. "Please, take a seat," he says, indicating a plain wooden chair in one corner.

Helen manages to keep from giggling, and takes his hand, then sits on the offered seat, spreading her skirts modestly. Both Andre and I reclaim our spots on our beds and the three of us share a long triangle of silence.

"So," Helen finally says, "what you boys doing? Reading?" She holds a lit cigarette and ashes out the open window.

"We are reading the gospels," Andre says. He pauses and glances at me. I notice his eyes are very blue. I'm not sure how I missed that before. "I am reading the gospels, anyway."

She taps her chin, her eyes darting around, clearly not listening. Our room is spare and I'm not sure what she's looking for. "You guys want to go out? Take a walk?" With a direct stare, she pins Andre in place. "See what kind of trouble we can get in?"

Andre sputters. In France, he once told me, the population has gotten so out of control that youths are kept separate until marriage. I wonder if he's ever really spent time with women.

"Helen," I say, clucking. "Leave Andre alone."

"Oh shush. I didn't mean anything by it." She laughs and arches her back. Andre's eyes look fit to burst before he closes them. "I'm a good girl, you know?"

I eye her cigarette and say nothing. There's nothing in the Bible about smoking or drinking that I can recall and my statistics class was clear: correlation implies nothing. God's law is less clear but still, I think Helen's safe enough. "I think I do," I say. "But why are you here?"

She doesn't hesitate. "I'm here," she says, taking another long drag, "because I got kicked out of another school. My fifth in one year. Instead of going to class, I hung out with older boys." Andre's eyes open wide and she glares. "I never did anything, though my parents didn't believe me. I'm a virgin." She looks back to me and continues, "But I like to have fun. After I got caught, again, they signed me up at my pastor's recommendation. To seed the galaxy." She grins, turns to Andre and says, "Seed."

Andre sputters and turns his face, muttering in French. "Allez, s'il vous plaît." When we don't respond, he tries again, "I am sorry, please leave." Pulling the covers over his head, he disappears from our view.

I laugh and help Helen back out the window, linking my hands and hoisting her up. When she's outside, she turns to me. "You'll have to tell me why you're here," she says. "I showed you mine, right?" She lights another cigarette and disappears into the night.

The next morning, I look for Helen after we get the boys up and moving. New Nazareth is like one of those towns in super-primitive Hollywood movies that they used to show very late at night: there's a main street and buildings on both sides for half a mile. Then, the desert (or in this case, the lush countryside – no metaphor is perfect) takes over and nothing is visible for miles. The hotel and small clinic aside, all the buildings are made of pre-fab, cheap materials – plastics are produced near the spaceport and shipped via barge, according to the manual – that are rapidly wearing down and have achieved weather-beaten status. Only the houses are well-made, small, ranch-style, built with lots of brick and stone. I imagine they'll get to the rest later.

A grocer, a hunting supply store for the herds of bison and countless deer, a tiny pub and a diner make up a majority of the storefronts. I look in the diner first, but see no one besides the morning janitor scrubbing down the plastic counter. "Have you seen a girl?" I ask.

He shakes his head and shrugs, pointing next door. "Thanks."

Outside, I bump into a man exiting the grocer's, upend his bag of miscellaneous goods: beans and bread, but also a flannel shirt, nails and red thread. After I help him gather it, we stand and I realise he's a big dude, six-two maybe, with a severely receding hairline, though he doesn't look particularly old. We play the changing directions dance for a few seconds, before he stops and tips an imaginary hat at me. He looks a little familiar. His eyes are dark brown and heavily-lidded; a tear-shaped tattoo under his left eye.

"After you," he says in a pleasant, deep voice.

I thank him and continue. I poke my head inside the grocer's and see a wisp of red silk in the corner of the room. I turn just in time to see a door "thunk" shut. The walls around it are lined with the random detritus I'm familiar with from the bodegas around home. Shady-looking food, clothing, soap, toys, a little bit of everything. Everything looks out of date and cheap. There are no supermarkets on Eden, obviously.

"Can I help you?"

The woman behind the counter wears a severe black dress and white bonnet and is thickly pregnant. Three small children, the oldest still an ankle biter, are behind the counter with her in a plain wooden playpen. The barest hint of a smile flickers across her face. Her fingers are long, bare of jewellery. When she stands, stretching, I see a red sash cinching her waist.

I approach, nodding my head in deference. "I'm looking for my friend," I say. "A girl."

"A stranger like you?" the woman asks. "A pilgrim?"

I shrug.

She purses her lips and shakes her head. "I have not seen any girl-pilgrims," she says. "Perhaps she is with her friends?" A heavy ledger is in front of the woman and she marks it with brisk pen strokes, dismissing me. I stand there, unsure of what to do. "Maybe you should return, little boy," she says without looking at me. "My husband will be stopping by shortly. It wouldn't do to be found alone with a married woman." She winks without humour. "Or any woman."

I back up and return to the sunshine. The street is empty, though I see a horse-drawn wagon leaving, heading back the way we came, laden with supplies. Purple light reflects off the big man's mask and cap-covered head. It all clicks: the big man exiting the grocer's is a white mask. What was he doing there, I wonder.

By the time I get back to the group, everyone's packed up. Helen is standing quietly with the rest of the Witnesses and when we make eye contact, her eyes laugh a little.

Andre grunts when I rejoin the throng. His eyes are bleary from lack of sleep; I heard him groan all night long and I knew what kept him awake, though I didn't share it. He said nothing about it last night after she left or this morning when we prayed silently at dawn. I wondered what his prayers were, if he asked for deliverance from impure thoughts, if God spoke to Andre. God never spoke to me, no matter how many times I asked for help. Jealousy nips at me again when I see his face – calm despite exhaustion – and I knew that God comforted him. He catches me looking and mistakes my expression for concern.

"I am well, my friend. Are you excited to be going again?"

I shake my head, unable to express anything.

Only two days later, we're stuck on the wrong side of the main artery of the Babylon, a Mississippi-sized tributary that segments half of the continent. The main river – Seraph – is twice the size; large enough that swimming across hasn't been done. I haven't seen it, but the manual implies that some whales swim it. Regardless, the rain that's coming down has flooded the Babylon well past its banks and we're stuck in our makeshift tent city eating cold beans and shivering in burlap.

After Andre leaves for prayer with a mumbled invitation that I don't bother to decline, my astra friend, in a burst of purple mud, darts in. His slick, oily "fur", after a quick shake, is suddenly clean and my tent – myself included – are covered in a thin layer of gunk. "Percival," I say through clenched teeth, "that was... unnecessary."

It watches while I clean my tent. The dirt here is different from Earth; grittier, stickier and it takes a lot of scrubbing and scrubbing. "You, my friend, take more work than any pet I ever had." Percival looks at me, cocking its head. When I continue, it licks itself clean with a long, beak-like tongue that I'm finally used to. "I had a dog back home. I named it Cameron."

There's some kind of commotion outside that I can hear through the deluge pounding on my tent, yelling and pounding, but I ignore it. "Cameron was a good puppy," I say, reaching into my knapsack for the hunk of bread I saved from lunch. I break it into little pieces and feed them to Percival. He won't take it from my fingers, but he doesn't seem frightened. "I got him a year ago. Or however long ago it was; I'm terrible at math, but I know it's been a long time, with relativity and all. You know about relativity, right Percy?"

The astrident doesn't respond and I sit down, suddenly tired. "They were going to take Cameron away at first, when my parents found out. But I threatened to run away and they backed down. I'd never yelled at them before." I'm done cleaning, my arms lightly marked with purple crud. I make patterns with my pinky, tracing rivers and swirls into my pale flesh. "They signed me up before I turned sixteen, before I could decide on my own. They were going to just send me to a camp to 'fix me' but instead, they sent me to another freaking planet." I reach out to Percival to pet him, expecting him to skitter away. And he does... but not until after he lets me touch his fur. It's not the most pleasant fur (it's not even really fur), coarse and waxy instead of slimy like I expected, but it's still a warm creature that I can pretend loves me.

Seconds later, Percival explodes back into the rainstorm, the flaps to my tent flying open. I'm soaked by the rain that intrudes, and a tall, brawny soldier strides in and shuts the flaps again. He's wearing a heavy black poncho and knee high galoshes. We've been handed that gear for when it rains, but they were passed out by the soldiers and then collected after the rain was over. I wouldn't have had any idea where to get them.

The man glances at me, though I can't see his face through the white mask. Normally I'd find that threatening – and I'm not exactly thrilled at the moment, especially with a face full of water – but nothing in the man's bearing seems threatening. His rifle is strapped to his back and his posture is relaxed. Even when he takes off his gloves and reaches up to take off his mask, his movements are slow and confident.

"Joseph," he says, looking into my eyes. He's got a

tear-tattoo under his left eye and I recognise him as the man I passed when we were leaving Nazareth, looking for Helen and now I realise where I knew him from before. The soldiers keep to themselves; they call themselves the Templars and they're a noisy cliquish bunch. We hear them in the night sometimes, hooting and hollering from their own camp a short distance from us.

I have no idea why he's here and just nod my head. A big juicy grin lights up his eyes and I notice that they're a deep green, with heavy lashes. The air in the tent gets a little bit thinner. "What's the tattoo for?" I ask, surprised at my boldness.

He blinks and then says, "Gang stuff. Not something I want to get into."

"Right," I say, thinking about conscripts and undesirables. Can I help you?"

The big man sits, his back against the flap. Wind howls, whipping detritus against the tent. Water drips somewhere steadily but I can't see it, just hear it ringing off something metal. My breathing has quickened but his remains steady. His eyes are reading me somehow. I don't know what he's figuring out as the minutes tick by but I'm not as nervous as I'd expect to be. I trust him somehow.

Finally, he seems to make some kind of decision as the wind intensifies and I hear a crack of thunder. "You're Helen's friend," he says. It's not a question. "I'm a friend, too."

I nod and say, "Joseph," even though he's already said it. I blush but he doesn't notice.

"There was some ruckus out there earlier. I assume you heard?" When I nod, he continues, "I thought so. Look, some people are going to come by in a little while doing a spot check." He scratches under his chin where stubble is becoming the first stages of a beard.

"They'll ask some questions about Helen; just play dumb, ok?"

I nod but my mouth already moves. "Why should I? Why are they coming around?"

He frowns and starts putting his mask back on. He's got a cross necklace around his neck, strung on red leather. The mask clicks into place and I'm staring at just the upper bridge of his nose and his eyes. "They don't know you're friends with her, alright? Just keep it simple and sweet." Standing, he adjusts his uniform. "My name's Jeckson. I'm Helen's friend, too, and we'll keep her safe, ok friend?" He puts out a huge hand for me to shake. "There are those who live a little closer to God."

"Sure," I say, mystified and overwhelmed by his presence, his physicality. His handshake is crushing and then he's gone, the screaming rainstorm flying around him. I watch him disappear, even as water rushes into my face and into the tent. He's gone but I keep on looking, long after I'm drenched.

I'm about to close the flaps when, out of the storm, two more soldiers appear, one tall and thin, the other of average height and strong-looking. They stop at the tent before me and one of them ducks inside while the tall one stands guard. I close my flaps and tap my chin, thinking about what my recently departed guest had said. Changing out of my wet clothes, I move quickly to restore my tent to a more pristine state, mopping up water with towels, cleaning the smudges of mud left by my guest.

Only when I finish do I get dressed again, am I aware of my excited state. I grab a pillow and a book and put them both on my lap, covering my embarrassment. I'm thankful I do, because the front of my tent opens without ceremony and I'm again hit with streams of water as the soldier silently enters, the tall man outside.

Unlike Jeckson, this one doesn't remove his gloves or mask, nor does he sit on the floor. Ducking his head slightly, almost able to stand in the fancy tents we've been living out of, he marches right back to where I'm sitting on my bed and plops down with a grunt. Then, the faceless white mask staring, he's silent.

I'm comfortable with silence, but this feels different, angry, the air thick and thin, hot and cold alternating. Not much time goes by, maybe a hundred heartbeats, when I croak out, "Is there something I can help you with?"

The man chuckles and removes one half of his mask so that it swings open, revealing a pale white face with a thin layer of white-blond stubble. His mouth laughs and he says, "I've heard about you, boy. Don't get any ideas about helping me with anything."

I don't speak, blood pounding in my ears. My head drops and I stare at the canvas beneath our feet. The man's boots tap, tap, tap and he continues. "Name's Jez and I don't want any funny business from you, am I clear?" When I remain silent, his hand comes and grabs me by the chin, forcing me to look at him. He's still smiling even when he squeezes hard enough for me to gasp. "I asked you a question little boy. I'll repeat it, *am I clear?*"

Gasping, I say, "We're clear. We're clear," and his hand falls away.

"Good to hear, boy. Like I was saying, no funny business." He leans back on Andre's bed and crosses his legs. "There was a girl in our camp earlier. We didn't get a good look at her, but she was doing something she shouldn't have been doing. Catch me?"

"Yes," I say.

"She was wearing muck-boots and a poncho – where she got it, I don't know – but under it, we think she had on a red dress. You know any of these girls what have a red dress?"

I think of the grocer and the glimpse of fabric I saw before the door closed and shake my head. "No sir," I say. I hear creaking and then silence. I look at Jez and he's frowning, one eyebrow raised.

"Yeah," he says, "no one has any idea." He stands up and strides over to the front. He takes one more look at me and laughs, "You tell me if you hear anything and I won't tell anyone about the funny business you had going on in here." He pauses. "Some people think they aren't spoken for. They think they get to make the choices."

My heart pounds in my chest and the air gets shimmery in front of me. "What are you talking about?" I ask, frantic, breath catching in my throat. He turns and mouths a single word: *funny.* "There wasn't anything funny!"

Jez chuckles and opens the flap, steps outside. He says something to the other soldier on guard and then sticks his head back in. "Just fucking with you, boy." And he's gone.

The beating of my heart takes a long time to quiet and the rain gathers in puddles in the front of my tent. I bail the water out, my hands shaking, and then tie the flaps loose before crawling into bed. I'm asleep by the time Andre returns from prayer.

"Shh." A hand presses down on my mouth and I bite, instinct taking over. "Ow. Shit. Shhh." The pressure on my mouth recedes and I recognise Helen's voice, her outline in the darkness above me. Andre's snores resound from the cot next to me.

"What the heck are you doing?" I whisper after she removes her hand. She keeps one finger to her lips that I can barely see. The rain has stopped but water drops from the tip of her nose in regular intervals, splashing into my mouth.

"Can you take this for me, Joseph?" she asks,

pressing something soft into my hand, her strong fingers gripping mine. "Just hold on to it for later, ok?"

"What are you doing?" I hiss, but she's already up and backing away, stepping lightly to avoid waking Andre. "What's going on?"

But the fabric rustles and a cool night wind blows in and she's gone, the tent closed behind her. I stick the dress under my pillow and turn back over to face Andre. His eyes are open and he's staring at me, a question on his lips.

"Talk about it tomorrow," I say to him and shake my head, confused about whether I'm still sleeping.

Andre purses his lips. "I heard talk about you," he whispers, "why you're here." The silence around us seems wrong somehow. I wait for it to start raining again, for thunder to strike the ground, churning mud over everything, for my little friend to come scurrying back into the tent. I am so tired of these conversations.

"Can't we talk about it tomorrow?" I ask, sleep coating my lungs. My eyes are drifting shut and my left hand sneaks under my pillow to touch the silk. I can't see the colour in the dark, but my fingertips reassure me that nothing is a dream.

The tent is full of silence for a hundred breaths or so and I let sleep take me again when Andre finally says, "I'm going to ask for a new tent, tomorrow. It's not right." He turns over, exhaling all his breath at once. "It's not right."

I open my eyes in the dark and listen to the non-existent rain. "I'm still Joseph, you know. And I didn't do anything." He doesn't respond and I'm asleep soon.

When we pack up the next morning, Hans speaks to the older ones. He has a very soft voice when he's not preaching, only a slight lilt to his consonants to colour his English. "The soldiers report a thief in their camp. They saw red clothing under rain gear." He pauses and rains his eyes to the clear purple sky. Only a handful of clouds dot the expanse.

The river is still swollen, but the ferry – made of rough-hewn wood and doctored with (precious, laboriously manufactured) sealant – is ready for us. Hans stands with his back to the riverbanks, his pure white robes reflecting the sun. His teeth are beautiful, his beard long and uncombed. He finally looks back to us and nods. "We must remain strong and pure, even here. The laws of man are less firm, but the laws of God?" He pauses to take a breath and bows. It's perfect timing and all of us – ten over the age of thirteen – shuffle our feet. I wonder how Helen feels but I can't risk peeking at her.

I do see Andre suck in his breath and glance to his side. But he doesn't do or say anything and soon enough, Hans continues.

"I have told our protectors to let us deal with this internally. I have prayed for guidance and I know whoever is guilty will come forth." His grin is huge. "I trust you all to hear God in your hearts."

We return from the riverbank and help the little ones finish packing camp. The ferry is waiting for us. I don't talk to Helen and she doesn't look at me. I remember covering for my sisters when my parents got after them. I'm comfortable with deceit like this. Smiling, I nod to Andre and he returns the greeting thin-lipped. I wonder who told everyone about me but I can't ask. The soldiers ring the camp, locking us down with their white masks and stiff posture. Again, I wonder why they're there, who they're protecting us from.

By mid-morning, I'm across the river and after lunch, we're on the road again. We don't stop for lunch, but push ahead. Helen draws up next to me.

She begins without preamble, without looking at me. "I hear talk about you going around town."

I stare ahead and simply say, "Yup."

"It wasn't me, you know."

"Nope."

From the corner of my eye, I see her smirk. "Glad you believe me. Hans has a ledger in his tent, you know. It's got little bullets points about each of us. Helen; 16; likely fornicator."

I can't help myself and swivel my head, jaw dropped. "What? Seriously?"

She shoos me, telling me to look straight and when I listen to her, she continues. "Joseph; 16; sodomist." I wince and she continues. "Jeckson; 25; devout Catholic; gang affiliations. Andre; 17; French." She laughs and ticks off half the camp: bi-polar, mental retardation; product of incest; crack addicted. "We're the flotsam of the Lord, Joseph."

Looking around at the wide-open world, I shrug and wonder if this is the land the meek were promised. She must catch my smile, because she hisses. Literally. "Joseph, do you have any idea what we're walking into? What kind of world we've been signed up for?"

"No," I say, though I'm starting to suspect.

"You need to look around," she says, taking her advice. When she blanches, shades her eyes and looks to the head of the caravan, I see a white-mask cantering toward us on his black nag. Only Jez has a black horse. "I'll see you later," she says and lets her wagon's speed fall off.

When we stop for the night, Helen doesn't come around, but Francois does, wriggling under my now-lonely tent. "Andre left, little buddy," I say. "Maybe I should give you a new name. What do you think?" The astra says nothing and waits for me to feed it. Before I can, my tent opens and Jez stands there.

He barges into my tent. "No funny business, boy," he says, slurring. "You know what's funny, is what's going to happen to your little friend." He offers me a bottle and when I decline, spits on the floor. "Suit yourself, little sodomite. Did you know that the first few colony ships were all men. Thousands of them, thousands of good Christian men and no ladies. I wonder how many of them became little sodomites like you." He belches and laughs. "The first few women who arrived were snatched up in minutes and forcibly married off. And I do mean force."

"I used to hate force," he says after a moment. "My foster parents didn't though, they loved it. And they loved to quote scripture while they loved force." He laughs and suddenly balls his fist, jumping at me. When I shrink back, he laughs. "They loved force a little less when I got bigger. Suddenly, the first time I hit back, I found myself on a ship across the stars."

My tongue feels thick, but I open my mouth anyway. "Is that why you got recruited to be a white-mask?"

He laughs. "White-mask? That's good. And maybe, but I like to remember it as a promise. I work for them, I stop the rebels from stealing our women, I get my own. Sounds like a deal to me."

Finishing the bottle, he tosses it at me. His backwash sloshes onto my hands. "Be seeing you little sodomite. Maybe sooner than you think," he says, winking. "Catamites are always welcome out here."

Trees – redwoods like the forests in northern California – spring up as soon as we're a few days away from the river. They haven't grown as tall as they are on Earth, but after a week of travelling through them, they're big enough to block most of the sun's rays. The wind can't get through the trees and the day feels heavy, still. The earth is dark purple and the astradents scurry through the shadows during the day, as well as night. Rain falls in gentle, never-ending waves.

Our wagons can only travel one at a time and

because it's the rainy season, we have to stop several times a day to push a wagon out of the mud. We're given more durable clothes – leather jerkins and ponchos – because of the incessant mud. When I'm not helping with the wagons, I'm alone. I'm told Andre discussed my "laying with men" in more specific terms.

Andre wasn't the most scintillating of conversationalists, but I miss him. Between him and Helen, I had started to create a sort of social group again.

Helen hasn't been around since the incident at the river. I think she knows how close she came to getting caught. I'm not sure what the worst case scenario is, however. She already got sent to another galaxy. What are they going to do? Kill her? She's already going to get married off as soon as we arrive in New Jerusalem, likely to an older man who "deserves" it. Talk is common now of what happens to women colonists; marriage is the best case scenario.

By midday, we're another day behind schedule, close to a week overall. Hans, after conferring with one of the soldiers, decides to call a halt. "We'll stay here for a couple days, see if the weather turns," he says, his fingers scratching at the underside of his chin as if by itself. "We'll get some extra prayers tonight and ask God to set us straight."

He says this last bit to me, then bites his lip. He looks embarrassed at least. I hear a snicker and I half-turn to see Helen, her face expressionless save for a very slight lip-nibble. Not sure what's come over me, I wink.

We break down the wagons and set up camp next in a big natural-seeming clearing, around a big stone fire ring. Our tents are set in concentric rings – Hans and the children closest to the fire, the soldiers in the outer ring, between us and the road. I'm pushed to the next-to-last ring, the closest to the armed men in those eerie white masks. There's only a handful of them and I know they aren't all bad, but the ones I don't know scare me so much more now that I've met Jez. They might be worse.

When we're done setting up, it's still light out for a few hours yet so I volunteer to gather wood for the fire. "Be careful out there," Hans says, his eyes not quite meeting mine. "Take a buddy, why don't you?" He looks around at the rest of the pseudo-adults and, whether by accident or design, Helen happens to step out of her tent, a sling in her hand. "Helen," he calls. "Go with Joseph to gather wood please. Maybe you can find a squirrel or something."

I ignore Helen's slight grin and stare at Hans. His broad smile fades a bit when I say, "There aren't any squirrels you know. Just the 'dents. The 'dents took them all out." His nod a few seconds later dismisses us and we head into the woods.

We're silent, waiting to get deeper into the shade, away from all the open ears and white masks. At least I am; I'm not sure what Helen's thinking. Her face is calm and her eyes wide, taking in everything. A brook babbles somewhere nearby and half-a-dozen deer bound away as we approach. Wildflowers and heavy mushrooms bloom at the base of the redwoods. Somewhere in the distance, a woodpecker works to get at the bugs deep in the mighty trees.

This is what heaven feels like, I think when a cool breeze makes it through the woods and tousles me. I smile and hum a nonsense song. "You're in a good mood," Helen says. "What do you have to be so thankful for?"

"It's a beautiful day," I tell her. "We're alive and God is right here."

She frowns, not looking at me. Now that we're away from camp, I look around for brush to use for firewood. Most is waterlogged but I gather a few likely looking pieces, grubs falling away when I lift them from the earth. Helen helps without complaining (my sisters would have moaned and cried about it) and her arms are soon full. When we're both at our limit, she turns and says, "Jez told everyone about you."

"I know," I say, "but where'd he find out?" Despite his book, I doubted Hans told anyone. But anyone could have known. My parents filled out a lot of forms to get me sponsored; questions about my sexuality had to be on there. Just like questions about Helen's proclivities must have been there. "It could have been anyone."

"It was probably one of the priests back at Trafalgar," she says, her voice full of bitterness. I wonder what stories have gotten out about her. "They gossip so much, it's crazy." She pauses and glances at me. "I figured you were gay, you know. That's why I wanted to be friends. You seemed as much out of place as me."

I shrug and don't respond, but I do slow down and look for a place to sit. There's a fallen tree, charred around the base, small holes where animals have gnawed into it and made homes. A flat brown head pokes out of it and chatters at me; I recognise my astradent friend. By the time we sit, "Archimedes" has disappeared back into the trunk. I drop my kindling. After a moment's hesitation, Helen joins me. She continues, "The soldiers have been gossiping about some outlaws that roam around." Her eyes are very big.

"Outlaws," I say, remembering Jez's drunken claims. What kind of outlaws could be on a planet this young?

"Not like the murder kind." She makes little guns with her fingers: *pow pow.* "More the kinds who go around recruiting pilgrims who think that maybe they want something a little different." She kicks at leaves and I see her socks. They're a deep crimson.

I let the silence drag. Some feet away, a bunny bursts

from some leaves and dashes, chased by a brown fox. The animals here have forgotten to be afraid of us. The woodpecker sounds closer now and in the brush behind us, there's rustling that grows by the second. "What's their deal?" I ask, taking care to keep my voice even. Helen's taking a risk, I sense, though I'm still not certain what kind.

She's about to answer, her mouth open, when a loud voice – one I recognise – says, "That's where you two are." I don't bother turning, but Helen does and her face goes hard, expressionless. "The sodomite and the Jezebel, buddies forever." Jez's coarse laugh sounds like a dog puking.

Helen stands and grabs the kindling she's gathered. I do the same, but slowly, my body tense. I've met men like Jez before. It doesn't take long to know how a certain type get their kicks. He reminds me of every bully I'd ever had. I hadn't had many, but the ones I did smirked his smirk.

Jez is alone and essentially unarmed, though his mask is still on. He's watching us move, his arms crossed, one hand tapping against his bicep. He's quivering with nervous tension and I'm suddenly scared. We're alone out here and he could do anything he wants to us. I don't hurry my pace, but I try to move more economically. Soon enough, we've gathered everything and setting off the way we came, past him.

He waits until we're nearly past him. One hand shoots out and grabs Helen's hair, yanking her head hard enough that she screams. It's unbearably loud and without thinking, I react. Dropping the kindling again, I launch myself at Jez, my hands scrabbling at his face. He laughs and bats me back with a slap.

The ground rushes up to meet me and I groan when my breath leaves in a rush. Trying to force my diaphragm to contract so I can breathe, I'm helpless, unable to speak while Helen swipes at Jez's hand. He pulls harder and she's bowed over almost double. He reaches to his mask and takes it off. Spittle dots his lips and he grins, showing all his teeth.

"You two need to understand the rules," he says. "We're your superiors, here and everywhere. We're soldiers of God." His inflection is matter-of-fact, like he's reading a list of ingredients. He releases Helen and just as she's standing, he kicks her feet, sweeping her legs from under her. "You will obey us; you think we don't know who's been stealing from our tents? Our liquor and cigarettes, listening to our conversations?" He crouches and speaks softly to Helen, but I hear, "We can't prove it and maybe you think that makes you safe. But it doesn't."

He looks down on me. I'm just getting my breath back when he places one foot on my solar plexus. He bears down just enough that I'm gasping. "And you, little sodomite, well, we don't like you much. And you have terrible taste in friends." He holds me in place and loosens his trousers. I close my eyes. Soon after he sighs and my face and neck is awash with warm, salty water that I don't think about. "This is what happens when you don't walk the godly path, little sodomite, little jezebel."

When he finishes, he zips up and says, "Better straighten up, kids. Once we get home, you'll see what the big boys are like. And they're not as nice as I am." I keep my eyes close, tears steady behind my eyelids, until I hear his footsteps fade into the distance. They stop and he calls, "Maybe sooner for you, little jezebel."

When I'm sure he's gone, I let the tears come, let them burn away the smell and shame. Helen's sobs trail away soon and then she's next to me, cleaning my face with her shift. She helps me to sit, her hand under my shoulders. "You see why 'outlaws' exist?" she asks.

When we get back to camp, no one seems to notice our state or that we've brought kindling. Hans nods but says nothing; Andre glares. The soldiers are off at their own fire pit, laughing. One of them – Jeckson – doesn't laugh, but looks over at us. I can't see his expression or even make out his eyes but I know he's trying to tell us something.

I see my first "outlaw" two days later. Nebuchadnezzar has finally decided to live in my caravan with me during the day and venture out during the night, only returning near dawn. My pet astradent is not a dog, of course; it doesn't sleep with me, doesn't allow me to pet and only sporadically allows me to touch it, but it has adopted something about me. Maybe it's just comfort and food, but it feels more like home. Sometimes, when it sleeps in the wagon, I can look at it and think about my home, about my sisters and my dog. For a short time, I feel normal.

The man's red bandana flutters when the soldiers shoot him. We're not prepared for it or, at least, I'm not prepared. We'd exited the redwoods earlier and were entering much warmer climates. It rained early but by midday a mist rose. It's quite beautiful really, flowers everywhere, rolling hilltops, lush green grass. We're lulled by the beauty of the day and the creaking of wagon wheels when the shot cracks out and a man half-a-mile away riding a horse falls over dead.

Clouds of dust are all we see of the horse by the time we get close to the dead man. The soldiers don't allow us too close but I see the dead man's cracked-open skull. His blood seeps into the purple ground, away from the bandana tied around his neck. One of the soldiers – not Jeckson or Jez or the tall one, but a fat, swarthy man – mutters, "Stupid. You don't know he's with them. Just 'cause he's got a red neckerchief...", before Hans hustles us away toward busy work.

The day no longer seems so wonderful and as I'm going over some bible verses with the little ones,

Andre walks up to me with one of the girls a few years younger than us. She's pretty, with small, grey eyes and a slim figure. She smiles at me when Andre introduces us. "May," she says, offering her hand. She tells the kids to scatter and they do, whooping as they go.

We shake and I mumble my own name while I search Andre's face for hints. He's playing everything close and he gives the barest nod to me. "How are you?" I ask. Helen, across the impromptu camp, sits very straight while she teaches her own group of kids, her eyes relentless, searching our trio as well as the dead outlaw a hundred feet away.

May bats aside my question with a flick of her hand and leans in close as Andre wanders away to converse with white-masks. She whispers, "Andre asked me to test you. On behalf of the white-masks. He's been kissing up to their leader for days. They don't trust you. Or Helen." I can barely hear her, but her breath is hot. "Gasp like I'm hitting on you," she says and I do. "Helen is my friend too. Look at my feet when I leave." She squeezes my bicep and backs away, turning her head and winking at Andre.

"Good to see you, Joseph," he says. "We have to be off." He guides May by her waist, leading her around to the far side of the camp, to one of the white-masks, half-hidden by a wagon. He bellows over to the kids I was teaching to come back and in a flood, they do. But before they crowd my vision, I see May reach down as if to scratch her calf, lifting her long dress so I see one brilliantly scarlet sock.

Later, May and Helen talk for a few moments during dinner. I'm separated by a dozen kids, two white-masks and thirty feet of bare earth and campfire, so I can't hear them. But they're not talking about boys, they're not talking about God and I'm positive I see a slip of raspberry binding Helen's ponytail.

Behind them, Jez watches me with calm, clear eyes.

He sees me staring and first frowns, then winks. Next to him, Jeckson meets my eyes and then nods. I have no idea what to think.

The falls are rather unspectacular; they appear on the map, but unnamed. Water flows by swiftly enough that ducks occasionally go over, only to spread their wings at the last moment and evade the jagged rocks. One, a squawky mallard, isn't so lucky, though thankfully its mangled body is hidden by the churning froth.

We're only a few days from New Jerusalem and we've passed several outposts, villages and even one mid-sized town. Another small group of pilgrims joined us a few hours ago. They started months before us. They'd have already gotten to New Jerusalem, but they all got sick at once: a bout of chickenpox laid half the children up. From what I hear, this happens a lot with pilgrims. One kid gets sick, they all do.

"Chicken pox?" Helen asks from where she's sitting next to me on my wagon. Now that we're so close and our group is so much bigger, watchful eyes are less prevalent. The white-masks didn't receive any reinforcements, so it's just the five of them for nearly two hundred. Jez has glared at me a few times but hasn't said a word. Andre has kept his distance, too.

When I was little, my sisters and I would ride around our neighbourhood on bikes. This isn't the same, isn't even close really, but it's something.

May's wagon sidles next to us and she shouts over the racket. "What are you two talking about?" We wave her off and she laughs. She spends a lot of time with Helen these days, as well as a shy, bookish boy and a pair of brawny, angry-looking fraternal twins from the new group. All of them wear small, hidden scarlet clothing. I can't imagine how the white-masks miss it.

I still have Helen's red dress. I keep it folded, inside

a pair of jeans. Nebuchadnezzar discovered it a few days ago and sleeps there. Helen saw it last night, laughed and told me to keep it until she needs it. I guess she'll know when that is.

Today, just before dawn, I thought I saw someone walking in the woods. They were only visible for a minute, just a head and shoulders in dark maroon leathers. No one else was awake and the mist that reminded me of home had swirled from the ground up. I blinked and the person in the woods were gone.

The falls are loud the closer we get. The day is almost done, the purple sun way past its zenith, and I'm ready to unpack for the night. Once we get to New Jerusalem and I meet with the rest of the Quakers, I'm hopeful that this nightmare of a journey will come to an end. That maybe, just maybe, my new clan will be tolerant, less suspicious, more willing to see God in me like I hope he is. Like I know he is. Despite what men like Jez think, I know God loves me as much as I love Him.

Helen nudges me and says, "Seriously, how did they get chicken pox?"

"How am I supposed to know? Dumb luck? Stupidity? God's judgment?"

She giggles. "It's probably the last."

We banter as we approach the falls. The water is fast, churning white froth from half-submerged rocks. From time to time, my eyes drift to the trees, searching for hidden flashes of auburn, magenta. Helen sees my search and purses her lips. Around lunch, I think I see the glint of sunlight off gunmetal, but it might have been anything.

The day lumbers by and despite the general foreboding in my heart, it goes by quickly. I'm enjoying myself in the sunlight and in Helen's company, away from judgment. Too soon, we're at the rapids and Hans calls for everyone to unpack. Helen clambers off my wagon and, just before she departs, zips into the open wagon. She's only gone for a second, but I know what she grabbed. "Is it time?" I ask, though I don't know exactly what's going on.

She jumps to the ground and nods. "Have you thought about it?"

"Yes." I pause. "No."

"Well, you should. We don't have much time," she says before running back to her own wagon, driven by some thirteen-year old she bribed with a smile.

At this point, after months of travelling, it only takes minutes to set camp how we want. I'm done and squared away quickly. "Be good, Nebuchadnezzar," I say to the sleeping lump in my jeans. I wash my face before I set off across the camp. I pass Helen and May – chatting quietly while setting their tents – and Andre, who's jawing with Jez. None of them notice me.

The edge of camp is close to the even, dirt road that appeared a few days back instead of the wilderness that we'd been travelling on all these months. There, by a lonely, isolated tent, is the white-mask who'd warned me, Jeckson. He's outside, digging at the earth with a large stick when I stop twenty paces away. An expression I can't quite process flickers across his face, but he beckons me to come closer with a large hand.

We face each other and I feel him sizing me up. When he relaxes, my own shoulders loosen. Finally, I say, "Are you wearing any red?"

His face stiffens and slowly he shakes his head from side to side. I continue, "You would though, if you could?"

Jeckson gives a fraction of a nod, before again shaking his head. A bead of sweat drips across his tattooed cheek. He says, "Maybe. I'd more say that I..." he wipes his brow and purses his lips, thinking, "...sympathise. Maybe someday, I'll feel more strongly.

But I have my own questions." He nods again and says, "You have some of your own?"

"When we get to New Jerusalem, some bad things are going to happen to the ones who don't get along, aren't they? To Helen and to me and to others?" I don't wait for him to nod. "I don't know what the colour signifies, why it was chosen, but it has to do with some kind of resistance, doesn't it?" I pause and take a deep breath. "This question is important to me. I might not be wanted or trusted around here 'cause I happen to like men, but I'm still a follower of Christ. And I need to know, are these 'outlaws' righteous? Do they still praise Jesus in every breath, in every action?"

Jeckson doesn't hesitate. "Yes, of course."

"Thanks," I say, and march back to the camp, aware of his eyes on the small of my back.

For the next few hours, I'm on high alert, watching every shadow, looking over my shoulder. Twice I think I see burgundy in the bushes, rose in the shadows, but when I look again, I see nothing but forest. The river itself gives up nothing, just the occasional leaping trout.

At dinner, I'm sitting on a stump near the river, eating from my plate of beans and meat when Andre walks past. He stops and glances toward me, meeting my impassive gaze. His lips twitch as if to smile or speak and I wait for him to say something. He looks away from me, at the white-masks laughing over a tin of beans, then back. His feet stutter-step and he clearly makes up his mind, because he frowns, lowers his head and keeps on going. I don't think about him very long, because I hear a scratching at the back of the stump. When I look down, Nebuchadnezzar is there, paws outstretched. I hang over a small portion of my meal and eat with my furry alien friend.

Nebuchadnezzar darts away as soon as the sun goes down and Helen and May (and the twins and the bookish boy) are all huddled around a fire, reading from the Old Testament. Jez and Andre are with the rest of the white-masks. Hans is giving a sermon near the falls, his back to the river. His voice rises and falls as a preacher's should and I relax. Nothing will happen tonight. How can it?

"And the Lord spoke to Isaac and told him to kill the fatted calf..." Hans and I tune him out. I'm familiar with the parable, but it's not one of my favourites. I prefer the prodigal son, though I can never figure out who I feel for the most. The father, likely. He just wanted his son back.

I don't want anything and I don't feel prodigal. If anything, I'm in the bosom of God himself and I have to assume He has a plan for me. Whatever it is, I'm ready to embrace it.

I try to catch up with Hans' sermon. We make eye contact and I think he smiles at me, though it's hard to see in the dim light that flickers off the running water and the ambient glow of the fire. I wonder if he approves of me, if he views me as someone to bring back to God.

I'm thinking about this when the first explosion hits.

Near the falls, a huge gout of water zooms dozens of feet in the air. Everyone screams, ducks and turns. The white-masks react quickly, the two on duty hauling out their rifles and pointing, the others running to their tents. They're the ones who are zapped first with a fancy taser-like dart that whistles as it flies from the woods. They fly off their feet and jerk on the ground, frothing, Jez with them. Some part of me realises that he and I never have a confrontation, no closure, not after this. He'll wake up, but I already know I'll be gone.

As soon as they hit the ground, Helen whips off her white robe, exposing the scarlet dress underneath that

I've been hiding under my pillow until just a bit ago; I knew it was there once she grabbed it; I knew this was coming, even if I didn't allow myself to know it.

The dress isn't tight or even particularly well-made, but it is bright. The other four follow her example: May has auburn slacks, the twins blood-red t-shirts. The bookish boy holds up wristbands of neon. I can't see who they're signalling to and neither, apparently, can the two white masks on duty. One of the white-masks yells in frustration and aims his rifle, swivelling to point at Helen and the others.

I'm not sure of much, just of my faith and that I have two friends in this world, an alien rat and Helen. It would take a lot, the world even, for me to give up either of my friends and I'm moving before I realise, off my little stool and sprinting. I hear a yell and a crack and I turn my head: the bookish boy twitching on the ground. Another explosion sounds in the water, but the white-mask doesn't even glance. I see Jeckson running toward the camp, his rifle unholstered but pointed at the ground. A taser hits him and he drops. The last white mask – the tall one with dead eyes – fires again.

I barrel into him, my head slamming into his solar plexus. For a moment, my vision fades to blackness, but I'm still flailing and screaming. He's strong, though and even though he's stunned, I know he'll overpower me. I bite and gouge and release my bladder as every frustration and fear and resentment comes boiling out. I don't hate this white-mask – maybe I would if it was Jez – but I hate so much and all I want is to love God and have others let me be.

My hands are around his head, smacking it against the earth when I feel someone grip me around the waist and pull. I tumble and stand, my back against the river. Andre stands in front of the fallen white-mask with a curl to his lips that I can't decipher. He's not afraid of me, exactly, but he also seems unsure what to feel. Behind him, three red-clothed forms run toward into the woods and disappear. They're supporting a slim form I know to be Helen.

Andre doesn't see them vanish. "You going too?" he asks, his face white.

I shake my head. "They're not going anyplace I understand."

He nods. "You can't stay here, you know. It is not for you," Andre says. I hear Jez's bellow. It's a matter of time.

"No, I guess not." There's a flash of brown fur around Andre's ankle and Nebuchadnezzar flies up my leg, his nails piercing my thin robes.

"What are you going to do?" he asks, but I'm already turned and diving into the river, Neb holding on to me with his sharp claws. I'm a strong swimmer, but the current is stronger and the roar of the falls drowns my hearing. I think of the ducks that fell, how they lifted their wings and flew. And I think of the one who died, crashing onto the rocks.

The water rushes in my ears, claws at my mouth trying to force its way in. I resist, allow the pummelling rapids to twist me around and tumble me end-over-end toward the falls. Nebuchadnezzar's claws dig into my leg and I latch onto the pain, the warm body pressed against me as the current takes me to the frothing falls.

I don't remember falling, but I know I do.

Birdsong wakes me. When my eyes open, the immense purple sky envelops me. I let my lungs fill with gentle breaths. I hear water lapping against the shore; I feel soft mud under my back and head, encasing my legs. For the first time since I've come to Eden, I feel at home.

I'm unsure how long I stay flat on my back as the

world fills me, but it feels like an eternity. Remembering biblical scholars at my old church debate about how long God's days are, I chuckle and sit up, soft mud squelching in release. "This is what being reborn feels like."

I take inventory and wince: my shoes are missing, my clothes are torn and mud-caked. Looking up and down the river, I have no idea where I am in relation to the falls and the rest of my former flock. It's a big world out here and I can likely walk for weeks in any direction without chancing upon a single person.

Of woodcraft, of wilderness survival, we were taught very little; the manual has no information other than identifying common poisonous plants. I wonder if it was deliberate, if by keeping us in the dark of how to survive without others, the powers-in-charge weren't trying to keep us in check. I shake my head at such a cynical thought, determined to reclaim the moment of tranquillity I'd just experienced. "Not very Christian," I murmur, "is it Nebuchadnezzar?"

I wasn't expecting a response, not really, but when my astradent friend emerges from the underbrush by the shore, I can't help but jump. He – I don't know when I assigned him a sex – limps, favouring his left-hind leg, but otherwise looks no worse for wear. He sniffs at me and settles onto his rear, sniffing the air between us. *Well, what now?* he seems to ask.

Before I can answer, I hear branches breaking and murmured conversation. Nebuchadnezzar dashes into the underbrush in a brown blur and I struggle to my feet, my fists balled. I hold my head high, ready for the white-masks or whatever to emerge and finish me. Instead, when a trio of crimson-clad figures emerge, my blood screams in my veins and I feel relaxation closer to joy. One of them, I realise when I stop hyperventilating, is Helen. She's wearing sturdy-looking leather clothes and her left leg is bandaged.

I want to rush and embrace her, lift her off the ground, but instead I lurch forward, my feet squelching in the mud, and extend a hand. "Hey Helen," I say, wincing at my awkward. Luckily, she brushes my hand aside, squealing when her arms go around me. My ribs ache from her squeeze and I'm sure she feels the same. "What are you doing here?"

"It took us a while to find where you washed up." She lets go and indicates her companions; they nod at me, one holding a rifle and scanning the area, his eyes darting birdlike, and the last is a blond woman, her hair back in a tight bun, tapping one foot and rolling a cigarette. "We couldn't just let you go."

"Where are the others?" I ask, thinking of the bleeding bookish boy.

She smiles. "May and the twins are on the way east. They've got a settlement in the mountains that's pretty self-sustaining. The white-masks don't go out that way. It's safe and the population is really growing. It's a viable alternative, you know?"

"I'm glad they're safe," I say, struggling to process. "I can't believe you came after me."

She pauses, frowns and then seems to force a smile. "We had to find you." She takes a breath and continues, "Dead or alive, you know? Christian burial or safe passage. None of us considered not looking." She pauses and adds, her lips forming the semblance of a smile, "Hans and the others left right away."

The others hang back, unsmiling but unthreatening. They're young, fit, weather-darkened, wearing muted shades of purplish-red, like camouflage. Visible crosses hang around their necks. "Safe passage where?" I ask, though I'm thinking of the scattered settlements they told us about when we first woke up, of individual homesteads and tiny hamlets scattered throughout the world. Maybe there's one on a beach somewhere, someplace similar to where I grew up, where quietly righteous neighbours will let me be.

If there isn't a community already, maybe I can start one myself. Not now, perhaps, but when I'm older, when I know more about this world and my place in it. At the least, it's a dream to hold on to.

Helen raises an eyebrow when the man, dark-skinned with bushy eyebrows, touches her shoulder and says, "We need to get out of their territory." She nods and grabs my hand.

"You'll come with us? They," she spreads her arms, "are good people. They're trying to make a new world." When her friends start to move, she pulls my hand, but I don't budge. "Please, Joseph? We've come so far." She lets go and takes one step back, toward the others. The man with the eyebrows shuffles his feet. I think about my sisters and how I still miss them and how Helen isn't one of them, not really. But they're dead and she's not.

Instead of responding, I kneel and search the shrub line around me. "Nebuchadnezzar?" I call. Something moves in the middle of a patch of poison ivy and I sigh. I walk toward it, making clicking sounds with my tongue. I repeat his name and hold my hand out into the ivy.

Time slows while I focus on the ugly snout that exits the ivy and sniffs at my hand. Someone mumbles about space rats, but I ignore it as Nebuchadnezzar edges toward my outstretched hand. I scoop him into the crook of my elbow. He's shaking, clearly nervous. "It's ok, buddy," I say. Nodding at Helen, I'm ready to go.

We set out, still heading south, following the river. At some point, I'm told, we're going to head east and then deeper south. Helen promises to tell me all about the red-clothes, about the resistance and more, but I don't promise to listen. I'll travel with them until I find where I'm going. Maybe they'll prove to me that they're true and right, but for now, it's unimportant. Helen smiles often enough that I know I've got a friend; Nebuchadnezzar settles down in my arm and sleeps. When the night comes we sleep around a small fire and I feel the beginnings of peace.

Beatrice et Veronique: Tunnel Panic!

Antonella Coriander

Beatrice and Veronique looked at each other in amazement. *Nothing* they knew was true? None of it?

"Okay," said Cornelia. "Now you know two things: my name, and that everything you thought you knew was wrong."

"Do I exist?" asked Beatrice.

"Do any of us?" said Cornelia with a bitter laugh. "All we can do is go on the probability that we do. *Cogito ergo sum*, you think, but who is the you? If you don't know that, what do you know?"

"What is this place?" asked Veronique.

"I'm sorry," said Cornelia. "I can't give you all the answers you want. It's not against the rules, exactly – there aren't any rules, exactly. But it could spoil the game."

She was making Beatrice angry. "Whose game? We don't want to play."

"That too would spoil the game." She reached into her coat again and brought out a small burner and a half dozen plastic pouches of various colours. "Let me get some food cooking and I'll tell you what I can. Cooky-do!"

She put the burner on the ground and activated it; it

glowed bright orange in the darkness, giving Beatrice and Veronique their first real chance to study their rescuer. She looked to be in her early forties, though that wasn't terribly helpful: by their century people were to some extent able to choose the age they wanted to look. Cornelia might be in her early forties, or she might be a teenager who wanted to look like she was in her early forties, for whatever reason. To Beatrice, though, the lines in Cornelia's face looked like they had been earned rather than etched. Despite her glib tone, the newcomer had a seriousness about her.

"How are your arms?" Cornelia asked Veronique. "Can you move them at all?"

"I can barely twitch them," said the thief. "I can't even shake my head to say no."

"Okay, I think I can help with that, while the burner warms up."

She took a malleable screwdriver out from her coat, and held it to Veronique's left shoulder for a moment. After looking at the digital readout in its handle, Cornelia asked if it would be okay to push Veronique's shirt off her shoulder. Consent given, she did so, and held the malleable screwdriver to the bare skin. The end of it twisted and turned and reformed into a notched disk, which when pushed into the skin seemed to act as a key. The shoulder popped out, leaving a gap of four or five centimetres. Cornelia leant closer and looked inside. It would have been impossible work in the darkness, but the malleable screwdriver sensed as much, and began to emit an inner glow. Cornelia seemed satisfied with what she saw, and after a few minutes' tinkering she clicked the shoulder back into place, pulled the shirt back up, and went back to her stool.

"They should work now," she told Veronique. "Give it a try."

Veronique lifted first one arm, then the other, opened and closed her fists, and turned her head from left to right. She was even able to suck her tummy in and out, which made them all chuckle.

She nodded with relief. "Thank you, Cornelia."

"No problem. I'm here to help. And it's nice when I can help without fighting."

Veronique shifted herself into a more comfortable position, drew her hands across her face to remove the detritus of the night's battle, and retied her braids.

Cornelia dropped the plastic pouches onto the burner, one by one, heating each until it, and the food within it, expanded to the required size and shape. The first three pouches produced hollow semi-spheres of bread. If it hadn't been for Cornelia's warning shake of the head, Beatrice would have stuffed hers down straight away; apparently robots *did* get hungry as well as thirsty. Or at least they thought they did. She was doing her best to stop worrying about that stuff. Just listen to your body, she told herself. Just get through this moment, and then get through the next. Eventually the worst of it will be over.

"If you eat that," said Cornelia, "you'll have nothing to hold the next bit!" The next three pouches didn't expand to form such regular shapes. "I have three options. I don't know when the two of you will eat again, or when you ate last, so you should get first pick. Roast chicken in gravy, lamb tikka, sweet and sour noodles. *Éspace de Gilligan* is open! What do you want?"

Veronique went for the lamb tikka, and Beatrice for the roast chicken in gravy, leaving Cornelia with the sweet and sour noodles. She did not seem unhappy with this result. She used a knife to snip off a corner of each bag and poured the contents into their bread bowls. The smell was wonderful, and for a second, for the first time since waking up on the island, Beatrice almost felt happy.

You're a robot. You can't feel anything.

I do, so shut up. And let me eat my dinner in peace.

She began to tuck in, nibbling a groove in the rim of the bread bowl and using it to pour a trickle of gravy onto her tongue. She closed her eyes and let herself fully experience the pleasure of good food.

"Thank you," she said to Cornelia. "So much."

"No worries. I have drinks too, though not enough to keep you going for long. You will need to find water in the morning." She balanced her bread bowl in one hand and took three small bottles out from her coat with the other.

"That's a very handy coat," said Veronique, after taking a long draft.

"People think I wear it to look cool," Cornelia said, "but inside it has zipped pockets from top to bottom. I'm ready for anything, as long as it gives me time to unbutton my coat."

Beatrice didn't want to speak, not while there was still roast chicken and gravy remaining in her bread bowl. Still, needs must when the devil drives you into a brick wall, and she asked: "Could you spare us any weapons?"

"Sorry, no," said Cornelia.

"The rules?"

"Yes, the rules."

They sat quietly for ten minutes or so while they finished their food and drink. The sun had not yet risen, but the stars had begun to diminish. The burner was left on, to keep them warm and provide some light. The crystal cuboids showed no sign of returning, either to resume battle or to recover their fallen comrades. Beatrice would never have admitted it, but she ate slowly to keep the moment alive. Whatever Cornelia had to tell them, it couldn't be good.

At last they were all finished. Beatrice and Veronique waited patiently for Cornelia to gather her thoughts. Eventually she was ready to speak.

"There is very little I can tell you, but I will tell you what I can. I asked you for your names not to find out who you were, but to find out if you were going to trust me. Like I said, I'm here to help, and that's easier with people who aren't trying to kill me."

"Who sent you?" asked Veronique.

"It doesn't work like that," Cornelia replied. "I won't tell you the whole sad story of my life, but I am lost in time. I find myself in places where people need my help, and I help them if I can. If I can't find anyone to help I try to have a good time – and that usually leads to someone needing help! But along the way I have picked a few things up about this universe of ours, and with you two I recognise the signs."

"What signs?" said Beatrice. "You're being so vague!"

Cornelia shook her head and pressed a finger to her lips. (Her own lips, that is. If she had tried it with Beatrice she would have needed a new finger!) "I can't travel with you, but I can suggest a direction for you. I can tell you that this island is under the control of a crystal wizard. You were just fighting her minions."

Veronique interrupted, frowning. "They did mention a wizard. And they said the dinosaur was hers too. So they were right? Is magic real?"

"You are going to have to make a lot of adjustments in the near future," said Cornelia, "and you are going to realise that the world is not what you thought it was. But this is a wizard in the technological rather than magical sense. This is all science, albeit of a very peculiar kind."

"And that's where you want us to go?" asked Beatrice. "After this wizard? We wouldn't have survived the battle with her minions without your help. We wouldn't stand a chance against a whole army of them."

"You reckon without your robotic nature and my malleable screwdriver," said Cornelia. Said item had suddenly re-appeared in her hand. "I can't give you any weapons, but I can remove some of the baffles blocking your innate abilities. As I have with you, Veronique. Can you try walking?"

Veronique looked angry. "I don't have any legs!"

"Try walking with your arms. Lean onto them and push down as far as you can."

Veronique clearly doubted the sense of Cornelia's instructions, but she gave it a try. She clenched her fists and put them on the ground, then tried rocking her body forward to balance upon them. She managed it for a second, but came nowhere near walking on them.

"Try again," said Cornelia. "And this time push harder."

She did. She was astonished to find that her arms began to telescope, internally at least – the skin remained unbroken, and seemed to stretch. In seconds she was striding around upon her elongated arms. The brush scratched against her now-bare forearms and the broken shards of crystal cuboids digged into her knuckles, but it was worth the discomfort to have her head back at its usual elevation. She would put her gloves back on before they set off.

"How is it?" asked Cornelia.

"Surprisingly groovy," said Veronique, who at that very moment balanced on one hand while reaching out to grab a branch with the other. In a flash she was up in a tree, and climbing to its topmost height. "I see fresh water. And a building!" she called, before climbing back down to sit beside them. "It looks inaccessible from here, but it must be where this crystal wizard is based. It shines like a glitterball falling into the sun."

"That's the one," said Cornelia. "And I know a way in. There is a tunnel, and in a moment I will give you directions to its entrance. The passage through the tunnel and your encounter with the wizard will be dangerous, but there is no other way of escaping this island. Not for you. But first" – she turned to Beatrice, malleable screwdriver in hand – "it's your turn."

Beatrice was taking small, careful steps in the darkness of the tunnel. She imagined falling over, becoming incapacitated. That would never do!

"How are you doing, Veronique?"

"Not too bad," replied the thief as she stamped along on her hands. "Thank goodness for gloves!"

Cornelia Gilligan had given them their instructions. If they wanted to leave this island they would have to make their way through the tunnels to the lair of the crystal wizard. They then had to get past her, either by force (that would fall to Beatrice) or stealth (Veronique's speciality), and throw a spanner in the works of the wizard's machinery. Or smash the machinery to bits with a spanner – whichever opportunity presented itself!

"I can barely see a thing," said Beatrice. "I don't see why Cornelia couldn't have given us a torch."

"The rules, I suppose."

"You say that like it's acceptable," said Beatrice. "It really isn't."

"No," said Veronique, "not acceptable. Ineluctable. Inescapable. Whatever's going on here, we've got to see it through. We'll get a chance to take our shot."

They had come to a place where a jagged emptiness dashed across the tunnel floor, as if it hoped they wouldn't notice it. They might not have done: it was barely visible in the faint light being emitted from the exposed machinery at the base of Veronique's torso. The gap was perhaps five metres across.

"Think you can get across?" asked Veronique. "I'm not sure my arms will stretch that far."

"I'll give it a go," said Beatrice. She pointed to her back and Veronique climbed aboard.

Beatrice took a dozen steps backwards, then ran at the gap. She planted her right foot at the edge and extended the leg as far as it would go, pushing the two of them out into space. Momentum kept them up in the air, but as her right leg reached its limit she wondered whether the left leg was going to reach the other side. She pushed it out, further and further. If she'd still had tendons they would have snapped a hundred times.

She felt herself begin to fall, pivoting on the planted right foot, and began to despair: by Veronique's light she could see the teeth of this hazard, a thousand jagged rocks ready to smash them both to bits.

But then her left foot slammed down on the rock of the gap's far side, and for a moment she balanced, catching her breath, whispering a million thank yous to her new body's manufacturer. The question was what to do now. Dig in the toes of her left foot and try pulling her body across?

Before she could ask the question, Veronique was in motion. She swung around from Beatrice's back and clambered along her left leg. Reaching safe ground, she grabbed a stalagmite with one hand and stretched the other hand out to meet Beatrice's. A big heave later and both were safely sitting on the far side.

"I don't know about that kind of thing," said Beatrice. "I thought these new powers would make things easier. Feels like they just encourage us into more trouble!"

Veronique laughed, but then went quiet, peering into the tunnel that lay ahead.

"What is it?" asked Beatrice, but Veronique held up a hand, tipping her head to listen more carefully. Eventually she returned her attention to Beatrice.

"There's something up ahead," she whispered. "I can hear tiny sounds of movement, and see tiny dancing lights."

Beatrice moved quietly to sit beside Veronique, facing in the same direction, so that she would see what her friend could see. Nothing at first, but after a moment she saw it too.

"More crystal cuboids?"

"I don't think so," said Veronique. "These look much smaller, and the cuboids weren't this nippy."

"Here's where I wish we had weapons."

Veronique stuck out her tongue. "Here's where I wish I had not been half-eaten by a dinosaur."

"You can still be fixed," said Beatrice. "All else fails, I'll give you one of my legs. Or at least a decent head start next time you steal from the Queen."

"Least you could do," said Veronique. "The very least."

The two stood, one on her feet, one on her hands, and they began to step slowly down the tunnel. Half a dozen paces on, the source of the lights became clear. Tiny jewels, much smaller than those that had crewed the crystal cuboids, scampered back and forth on multiple minuscule feet. They came in all colours (red, blue, green and white predominating) and a dozen shapes (arachnid, beetle, scorpion, centipede, stick insect), and all shone with a queer inner light.

Beatrice and Veronique would be able to stride more confidently now, with the natural light of these things illuminating the way. But would the tiny minions attack?

Veronique balanced on her left hand and used the right to gather a loose stone from the broken floor. She tossed it in the direction of the creatures, not so hard that it would smash them – for all she knew these might be nothing to do with the wizard! – but fast enough to give them a fright.

And it did – the creatures scattered at the stone's approach, like children from a jellyfish at the beach. But once the stone's threat was passed they returned to their work. What that work was, Beatrice couldn't tell, but it seemed important to them.

"Babies?" asked Veronique.

"Possibly," replied Beatrice. "But these are gems, not mammals. Perhaps this wizard can animate gems, and the larger they are, the more intelligence he can give them. The big ones become cuboids, or even dinosaurs, while these littler ones are the worker ants."

"It seems safe to advance," said Veronique. "I think we should. But let's try not to step on them. They might leave us alone, but if we begin to cause trouble they might call for help."

The police officer agreed, and they continued, picking their way carefully through the minions. Close up, they could see that the legs emerged from a cradle in which each crystal sat, rather than growing directly out of the crystals. The tunnel itself, which twisted back and forth and round and up and down as if they were walking the route of a celtic sigil, began to explain the creatures' activity: an apparently delicate webbing that coated the walls became apparent. It glowed in the dark, a bright crosshatching of lines over every surface. The further into the tunnel they went, the more solidly the webbing covered the wall, and the fewer minions could be seen at work.

At a certain point Beatrice realised that this could no longer be called a tunnel. It was a corridor, gleaming with light, worryingly artificial, beautifully clean. Except for the trail of foot and hand prints they had left. So much for stealth!

"I think we're in the wizard's headquarters now," said Beatrice.

Veronique nodded. "Though it seems strange to say headquarters. A wizard should really have a castle."

"Or a tower."

"Yes, a tower would be good. This just looks like, I don't know, a hospital, or a military base."

"With crystal wallpaper," said Beatrice. "Are you ready to do this?"

Veronique shrugged. "Do what? Walk along this corridor a bit longer? Sure."

"You know what I mean."

"I think so," said Veronique. "Are you? Are you ready to fight, if we have to?"

"You might as well ask a panda if it's ready to sit around eating bamboo," said Beatrice. "Or a banana if it's ready to be peeled. I don't like violence, but what must be, must be."

"For a minute there," said her friend, "I thought you were going say that you don't like violence, but you're very good at it."

"I was, but then realised I was half-quoting a TV show and felt silly. But now I wish I'd stuck with it. What must be, must be. Not a great line for an action hero." Beatrice stretched her arms and legs. No functionality problems yet, so far as she could tell.

"Will this really get us home?" asked Veronique, as they set off again.

Beatrice thought about it for a moment. She wanted to say yes. As a police officer, keeping people calm was a big part of her job. But was she still a police officer here? Was she even the same woman? Or did she just think she was – *feel* she was?

But when she thought back to their conversation with Cornelia Gilligan, she couldn't remember the mysterious woman ever actually saying this mission would get them home. She did say it would get them off the island – but that wasn't the same thing, was it? This might still be the early stages of the game.

The very thought made her angry. She was a police officer: rules were her job, her passion. They existed for a reason, for everyone's benefit. If this really was a game, and it was a game that had rules, it was utterly unfair to expect her to play without knowing what they were.

It was rude, that's what it was.

And if she ever met the person who put her in this situation, that was what she would tell them.

Ahead they could see that the corridor was reaching its end, and so began to step more quietly. Who knew what would be waiting for them? As they got closer, Veronique had an idea. Rather than handwalking, she reached up and grasped a handhold of the ceiling. Though the crystal webbing at this end of the tunnel had hardened, she was able to force her fingers through, stretching the threads, letting her swing instead of walk.

It looked like the corridor would disgorge them into a small, rectangular room, but from here they couldn't be sure. Veronique swung ahead of Beatrice, and motioned for the police officer to wait. It made sense. If anyone was guarding the entrance, they'd probably have eyes set at ground level. Though the corridor's ceiling was not high, it might be enough to give Veronique a few seconds of advantage.

She centimetred forward.

What. Was. That?

It had grabbed Veronique before she had time to process what she had seen. It ripped her from the corridor into its chamber – or most of her, at least. Her fingertips were left behind, held fast by the crystal webbing of the corridor's ceiling. Perhaps she would have screamed with the pain of that, if she hadn't already been slammed into a shining bright wall. It splintered under the impact, and she felt those splinters bury themselves in her body.

Beatrice took a deep breath and ran into the room, hoping she could at least give herself a chance to see what she was up against. She didn't close her eyes as she ran, but she wanted to.

Running so fast she almost thumped her own head, she hit the far wall without being crushed, then turned to see.

The previous crystal creatures they'd encountered had resembled recognisable creatures from earth. This one did too, not that she realised at first. It was a gigantic angler fish, its crystal form stained purple and green, crumbling at the points where those colours were most dark. It stood not on legs, but rested upon irregular extrudences from its bottom half. The chamber had clearly once been a laboratory of some kind, but little evidence of that remained intact. Half a test tube here, a broken bunsen burner there. The revolting creature had begun to smash this chamber up long before they arrived.

But now it was smashing Veronique. It was holding her – no, it wasn't that. One semi-molten fin had attached itself to her, and flapped horribly back and forth, slapping her again and again against the wall, the floor, the ceiling. Like a savage parody of a woman with toilet paper stuck to her shoe.

There was nothing for it, thought Beatrice. What good was a robot body if you couldn't knock it about a bit? As she threw herself into the fray she tried not to think about the likelihood of ever being repaired.

She rammed her extended arm into the pilot fish's crystal eye. The effect was a satisfying crack, and the creature opened its mouth to wail like a midnight cat. But her hand didn't come free. It wasn't just stuck – it was being drawn in, as if sucked into quicksand. This thing was corrupt, damaged, breaking down. Too slowly to help, though. It was still plenty strong enough to do for them.

The creature had temporarily ceased its cruel battery of Veronique, but as its fin drooped down she showed no sign of waking.

"Wake up!" shouted Beatrice. "Veronique, I need you!"

Veronique's eyelids shifted as her eyes moved, but they didn't open. Beatrice's arm was in the pilot fish's eyesocket up to its elbow, and the foul beast was snapping at her with its grotesque lower jaw. Attempts to retract or extend the arm had no effect, and she had no option but to swing up on her own arm, landing on the thing's head. The trapped arm creaked mournfully, and a second later she was overwhelmed with reports of pain.

The pilot fish threw its head up and Beatrice's arm came off.

She rolled down its back and landed heavily on the floor.

Beatrice was in agony, but she had given the thief the time she needed. Veronique was awake.

The thief's face was cracked from side to side, but her eyes were open and now with both hands she grasped the fin that held her. She put all her robot strength into it, and was rewarded with a satisfying shattering. She fell to the floor, part of the fin still stuck to her, then used her hands to roll herself over to Beatrice.

"We need to get out of here," Veronique said quickly. "We can only slow this thing down. We can't stop it."

Beatrice kicked herself for not having thought that first herself. In her line of work she was used to dealing with threats, neutralising them, not escaping and running away. But no civilians were here – no public to protect.

"Over there," said Veronique, pointing to a pile of rock and crystal in one corner. Beatrice hadn't noticed, but behind the debris could be seen the barest outline of a door. Maybe this thing had been sealed in here, or maybe it had sealed itself in, but that was their best way out.

"Okay," said Beatrice, getting to her feet to face the creature that now faced them once again. It held back, shivering, apparently aware it faced a foe that had hurt it once already. "I will distract it, you clear the way."

Veronique nodded. "Go for it. I'm ready."

Beatrice knew Veronique wouldn't start work until the pilot fish was looking the other way – at the door with her back to it she would make too tempting a target. This was good. She had someone to protect. A dangerous, unpredictable enemy. This was what she had trained for.

She ran at the pilot fish, swinging her one remaining arm to whack it across its one remaining eye. This time she was careful to catch it a glancing blow; she wouldn't get caught that way again. Still, she hit hard enough to splinter its eye, and as she let herself slide under its head the fish was clearly at a loss.

Problem was, it couldn't see now, so wasn't following her, and if it charged it would be right at Veronique!

Beatrice leapt up to grasp the bright bulb that dangled from its forehead. As the fish bellowed screechily in pain, she twisted and pulled it towards her. The creature turned, more quickly than she had anticipated. Its grotesque head knocked her flying, and she found herself back at the entrance to the corridor, flat on her back and gasping for what she was programmed to think of as breath.

But on the far side of the smashed-up laboratory she could see Veronique pulling at the rocks that blocked their exit. Selfishly, Beatrice couldn't help wishing that Veronique would throw a few of those rocks in the direction of the giant crystal pilot fish, but that would have defeated the point of the exercise.

And Beatrice was getting an awful lot of exercise!

The pilot fish was charging her now, even angrier than before she had smashed up its eyes. She rolled back into the corridor, avoiding the slap of its unbroken fin by a millimetre.

"Good grief, you're a naughty one!" she shouted. "I'm going to have a word with your mother."

The pilot fish howled so loudly that she saw crystals cracking at the back of its foul mouth. Like the crystal dinosaur, this creature did not seem to have the intelligence of the crystal cuboids. Perhaps it was down to size, that at a certain point the needs of a gigantic autonomic nervous system precluded the capacity for intelligent thought, reasoning, and obnoxious threat-making.

But it had responded to her words. As long as she stayed far enough back, she could keep it safely occupied here while Veronique did her work.

"You deserve a jolly good spanking!" she shouted, to its obvious displeasure. "Call yourself a fish? Bet you've never even been in the ocean!"

The fish decided to show Beatrice that she had underestimated its reach. Maybe its fin couldn't reach her back there in the tunnel, but it had another weapon: a tongue, that flicked out to wrap around her waist.

"Gah! Do pilot fish even have tongues?" shouted Beatrice, determined to stick to the job even if it hurt. "That's cheating! Or maybe not! I don't know! But it's definitely disgusting!"

She hammered at the crystalline tongue with her arm, but without effect, and she was getting dragged towards the creature's gaping, ghastly mouth.

Beatrice leant back against the tongue and jumped up to plant her legs on either side of the creature's mouth. She braced herself against it. "This would be a lot easier," she yelled, "if you gave me back my other blinking arm!"

It didn't seem interested in her thoughts on the matter.

The pull on her waist was growing stronger as the tongue wound in, and soon she would have to choose between having her waist crushed and letting herself be pulled into the mouth.

A fine pair of choices!

"I will have you fishy / on a little dishy / I will have you fishy / when the boat comes in!" This savage breast was not for soothing! Perhaps it was the subject matter. She sang a childhood song of her own composing. "I like dancing / I like singing / I like bells / When they are ringing!" The fish just seemed angrier, twisting its head from side to side as if that would help get her into its mouth. She hoped it wouldn't start smashing her against the wall as it had Veronique.

Her friend had now almost completely cleared the door, and was using one hand to move the rubble while the other searched for a way to open the door. There was no handle. If the door had once opened automatically, they might well be stuck in here with this angry blind fish.

"How's it going?" she shouted to Veronique. "Answer with your shoulders so you don't attract its attention!"

Veronique shrugged and continued with her work.

The strain on Beatrice's mid-section was now excruciating. If she had still (ever?) been human, she would now be dead. The rough crystal tongue would have ripped through human flesh like an egg slicer's wires through a boiled egg. As it is she felt her pseudo-flesh coming away from her metal skeleton.

"Hurry up, Veronique!"

The thief waved. Somehow she had got the door

open a crack, and was pulling hard to get it open all the way. She could only use one hand for the job – the other was needed to give her something to pull against – but it was nearly time to go.

How to get away from the pilot fish?

Preferably in one piece.

Beatrice had been a keen gymnast at school. She hadn't been on the horse or parallels for a good few years, but police work being what it was, what she'd lost in flexibility she'd gained in strength and stamina. The tongue wrapped around her waist prevented her pulling away. She doubted it could be so strong across its width. She bent over, forming a crab over the creature's mouth. That let it draw its tongue further in, but never mind that: between her two feet and her good arm she was in a strong position, and now she began to circle anticlockwise, twisting the tongue around and around. The tongue now became her unwilling assistant, keeping her from falling when she was upside-down. Round and round she went, the twists spiralling into the fish's mouth, the gaps between them shrinking, the twists getting smaller and harder. She kept turning the screw.

The giant crystal pilot fish began to scream. She was right in the way and could do nothing to protect her ears, so she tried to enjoy it for what it was: a sign that she was winning.

Veronique now had the door half-open, and that was probably as far as it was going to go – it was supposed to slide back into the wall. She lifted herself up and palmed over to Beatrice and the fish. She couldn't help Beatrice directly at first – the creature had dragged her from the tunnel and was still facing that way, its bulk between them (though of course she could still see Beatrice through its crystal body, or at least those patches of it that were not disgustingly corrupt).

She pulled herself up onto its tail and climbed across its body. Its putrid crystal scales tried to adhere to her hands, and its dorsal fin flipped from side to side, doing its best to get her. It would have been pathetic if it had not been so dangerous.

She was now in position. She settled her torso down onto the back of the fish's head, sickened by the squish but knowing it had to be done. She extended her arms to rest on Beatrice, one on her left shoulder, the other on the opposite hip.

Beatrice stopped spinning, and the two of them shared a look.

"Now push!" shouted Veronique, a fraction before Beatrice would have said the same thing.

Veronique pushed, forcing her arms to extend against the pressure, trying not to think about the crystal scales grinding against her waist. Beatrice pushed too, with both legs and her arm, pushing back against the tongue, which was now twisted and knotted along its entire length.

Had Beatrice done enough to create a weak spot? Would they be strong enough to break the tongue entirely? Having broken the tongue, would they reach the exit safely?

The answer to all three questions was yes.

Accessing the Future: Kathryn Allan and Djibril al-Ayad

Interview by Stephen Theaker

I interviewed Kathryn Allan and Djibril al-Ayad while they were in the midst of a highly successful campaign to crowdfund a special anthology of disability-themed speculative fiction, Accessing the Future, to be published by Futurefire.net Publishing. Though the campaign is now over, I think our readers will be interested in how they went about it. The anthology is currently open to submissions.

Hi Djibril, Kathryn. What made you decide to produce this anthology? What are your goals for it?

Djibril: Thanks, Stephen. This anthology will be the third produced under the aegis of Futurefire.net Publishing (after *Outlaw Bodies* and *We See a Different Frontier*), and all three are concerned with social-political speculative fiction from the perspective of under-represented viewpoints. The vast majority of the stories we have published reflect the understanding that oppressions are intersectional: so stories about imperialism recognise the fact that colonial oppression is closely tied in with gender oppression, with racism, homophobia and ableism. An anthology that takes as a starting point the marginalization of people with disabilities (both in reality and in literature), also from an intersectional angle, is a close fit to our aims as a press. We hope to raise enough money to produce a full-size, professional rate-paying, properly distributed anthology on this theme, with authors from a wide range of backgrounds and perspectives.

Do you feel that disabled people are under-represented in sf at the moment? If so, would you take the excuse that medical advances may leave fewer people disabled in future?

Kathryn: I would say that realistic representations of people with disabilities are few and far between in SF right now (and have been since the inception of the genre). There are many, many SF stories that address disability in some way but for the most part, those depictions are negative, poorly thought out, and insulting to people with disabilities. The idea that medical advances will "erase" or "cure" disability in the future is extremely dangerous and harmful for two main reasons: (1) it ignores the fact that disability is a social/medical construct (i.e. people create disability through language and medical practices, by environmental, social and political barriers to access), and (2) it tells people with disabilities today, "it's better if you didn't exist." Disability will always be with us if we continue to promote an idealised notion of "normal" – we need to recognise that human bodies exist on a spectrum of physical and mental difference, and that people of all abilities deserve the same rights, freedoms, and access to the resources required to live out the lives of their choosing.

Much sf deals with individuals dealing with physical adversity or communications difficulties, albeit because they are in non-terrestrial situations – do you think that makes the genre naturally suited to addressing larger issues around disability?

Djibril: Maybe, yes. For me, though, the interesting thing about science fiction/speculative fiction is the social-political side of the genre. I see SF not just as a medium for high-tech adventures, for world-changing cyberpunk or magical advances, but also and especially for explorations or imaginings of what *we* might become as the world becomes different in various ways. A world in which society or some societies respect and give access to people with disabilities, as well as other marginalised groups, is as mind-blowing and science fictional as a world with space elevators or teleportation technology. And the interplay between the two is the best of all – how does technology enable and lead to better society? How does a more enlightened society develop different priorities for technology and better uses for communication, space travel, replicators...?

Fans of Doctor Who could argue that Davros is one of the greatest television villains of all time, but his name gets thrown at wheelchair users as an insult. Then there's the Mekon, mutants, cyborgs – should we be more uncomfortable about the association of disability with villainy in science fiction?

Kathryn: Absolutely! Davros is an excellent example of how disability is used as a sign of villainy and evil in our media, especially in science fiction. We should not only be more uncomfortable about the association of disability with some sort of moral flaw or failing on the part of the disabled person, we should be calling such images out when we see them (as we do for racism, homophobia, sexism, classism, etc). As you point out in your question, these kinds of hurtful representations impact the lives of real people (e.g. a wheelchair user being called Davros). It is simply not okay for the science fiction universe to be populated by people with disabilities who are either (a) evil or (b) to be pitied and "cured". These kinds of representations need to change: everyone deserves to see themselves, as they are (and not as cartoon-like villains), in the stories they love to read and watch.

Where should we look for more positive portrayals of disabled experiences in science fiction? Are there SF books and stories that are well-regarded in the disability community, but haven't had the same impact in the sf field?

Kathryn: I recently wrote a post for Pornokitsch's "Friday Five" column on positive representations of disability where I pointed to the work of writers like Larissa Lai, Jacqueline Koyanagi, Morgan J. Locke, James Patrick Kelly, and Nalo Hopkinson. I think it's important to keep in mind that a writer might put out a book that has a realistic or "positive" depiction of disability but it's not marketed that way. The disability community is quite diverse and I am not familiar with every part of it (my little corners exist as part of the larger SF and scholarly communities) but there are certainly novels and movies that resonate more strongly with some people with disabilities than others. One fantastic resource for people who read YA literature, for instance, is the Disability in Kidlit blog – you can find excellent reviews and discussions of the portrayal of disability in the YA market there.

Some crowdfunding for books runs aground on the criticism that it's now possible to publish book in print and ebook without it costing the publisher a penny in production costs. Why do you think the Future Fire's projects have managed to escape that trap?

Djibril: Ha! – primarily because we've never raised enough money to completely cover our production costs, for one thing. But seriously, Futurefire.net is not and never will be a profit-making press: any further income we make after cover our costs will go back to the authors. The idea that there are no production costs at all is a fallacy: yes, you can publish via a print-on-demand supplier (as we do); yes, you can hand-craft ebooks using XHTML and Calibre (as I do), but that's not cost-free. Proofreading and copyediting take time; ISBNs and other production/distribution set-up costs money; marketing and review copies cost money. Even a modest, home-brewed anthology has several hundred dollars worth of set-up costs to recoup from sales. (And all this is without factoring in what we pay the authors.)

Why is it important to you that this be a paying publication?

Djibril: From a very selfish perspective, offering a professional rate of author pay is essential, because you receive many more stories this way; most top-notch authors won't write for free, but even that aside, you need a slushpile of *at least* a hundred stories from which to select 12–15 great pieces for a themed anthology. On a more principled note, though, it's important to pay authors a fair rate because writing is hard, it's feeding your own blood to a beast that maybe no one else will ever love. Writers deserve to be paid (and this is the editor of a 'zine that pays token or "semipro" rates speaking). Especially since we are hoping to receive many stories from authors who are underrepresented in speculative fiction – people from outside the Anglo-American world, people with disabilities, and so forth – many of these people are already financial disadvantaged, so paying them a fair rate for their fiction is even more important.

How do you approach the creation of perks for funders of your Indiegogo project? Where have you seen other projects go wrong? Has the good track record of the Future Fire in putting out its crowdfunded books, and the good reviews they've had, helped with the subsequent projects?

Djibril: We're by no means authorities on good crowdfunding practice, but I can say that I've learned from my own mistakes with a previous campaign. The first is that a four- or six-week fundraiser run is not a long time, so you have to work *really* hard to get the word out to all the communities who might be able to help. The successful projects are the ones who have tapped into the enthusiasm and support of their networks of collaborators and allies to help with spreading the word, writing or hosting blog posts, and even providing some of the higher level perks (like the story critiques, book bundles and Tuckerizations in our campaign). And yes, I think the success of previous publications both helps with our reputation, our reach and visibility, and increases the size of our network of friends to call on for help.

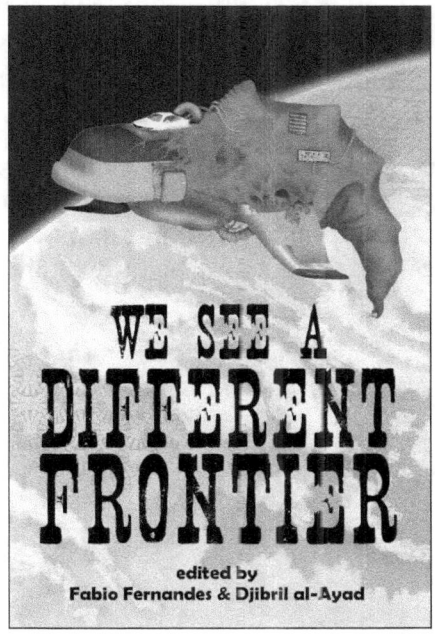

When the book opens to submissions, what kind of stories will you be looking for? And what aren't you looking for?

Kathryn: We definitely don't want stories of "cure" or that depict people with disabilities (visible or invisible) as "extra special" people that are inspirations to the able-bodied. We want to read stories that place people with disabilities at the centre as three-dimensional characters (with strengths and flaws). We want stories that are informed by an understanding of disability issues and politics, and that are intersectional (addressing race, class, gender, sexuality, etc). We want submissions from writers that think critically about how prosthetic technologies, new virtual and physical environments, and genetic modifications will impact human bodies, our communities, and the planet. We want to know: "What does an accessible future look like?" We want to read submissions from as many voices as possible.

When do you hope the finished book will be available?

Djibril: Our current timescale is for mid-2015; slightly earlier for reviewers and backers of the fundraiser. We're not committing to anything right now, but that's a likely target. You'll certainly be hearing from us when it is!

The anthology is open to submissions till 30/11/14:
http://futurefire.net/guidelines/accessingfuture.html

The Quarterly Review

Reviews by
Stephen Theaker,
Jacob Edwards,
Rafe McGregor,
Tim Atkinson
and Douglas J. Ogurek

Adventures with the Wife in Space

Review by Stephen Theaker

"... imagine if you could convince someone who hasn't seen the episodes to sit through them all? Someone who wouldn't know if a story was supposed to be good or bad before they'd even sat down to watch it; a person who didn't know what was coming next; a person who'd agree to watch the whole thing with an open mind and without prejudice. That's where you come in, Sue." In 2011, Neil Perryman persuaded his wife Sue to watch all of *Doctor Who* from start to finish, going so far as to watch fan-made reconstructions where the originals remain lost. While the viewing marathon was underway, one or two stories being watched a night, Sue's reactions and ratings were being recorded on a blog, *Behind the Sofa*, quoted here in small chunks. **Adventures with the Wife in Space** (Faber and Faber, ebook, 3179ll) is the story behind this adventure.

I found that a bit disappointing, in that I was more interested in reading about the adventure itself. But that's the blog. This is more *The Making of Behind the Sofa*, a behind-the-scenes book, packaged in a way to make it seem of more general interest. More than the story of watching the series, this is the story of Perryman's relationship with the series, and although he's a few years older than me (his first memory – "of *anything*" – is from the month I was born: the drashig in "Carnival of Monsters"), it's one very similar to my own. Love for the Tom Baker years, interruption during the Davison years (rugby for him, cubs for me), not watching much of Colin Baker, and then, at university, realising that he had missed the renaissance of Sylvester McCoy's second and third years and that leading back into enjoying the programme as a whole.

This will be an enjoyable if unsurprising read for fans of *Doctor Who*, and it may also appeal to fans of Nick Hornby; it reminded me a lot of *Fever Pitch*. But it's not essential, and those intrigued by the book's pitch who haven't heard of the blog will probably be disappointed by what's not here. In the early chapters I was thinking, okay, that's enough build-up, let's get onto watching the episodes, but it never really happens. Plenty of life, but could have done with more wife. ★★★☆☆

Buffy the Vampire Slayer Omnibus, Vol. 6

Review by Stephen Theaker

The seven volumes in this series look very smart lined up on my bookcase, but that made me forget that I hadn't yet read **Buffy the Vampire Slayer Omnibus, Vol. 6** (Dark Horse, tpb, c.400pp) (or its sequel), so I've put that right with great pleasure. Taken as a set, the seven omnibus volumes make a fantastic companion to the television programme, especially since their contents have been arranged in chronological order. The stories in these issues come from around the time that the Initiative was in town, so Buffy is dating Riley, Spike has a chip in his head, Willow is exploring witchcraft and romance with Tara, and Xander is with Anya. On television that felt like a sad time in the characters' lives, even if they were all falling in love, because Buffy, Xander, Willow and Giles, the original gang of four, were drifting apart, and frequently unhappy with each other. That made perfect sense in the show, but it's nice that here in the comics everyone is still good and chummy. The writers include Christopher Golden, Tom Fassbender, Amber Benson and Jane Espenson. It's odd that the kind of three-issue stories that seemed trivial when gathered together in flimsy graphic novels of under a hundred pages are satisfyingly substantial when run together as big, long stories in these books. It helps that this volume comes from the later, better period of the comic. The art, mostly by Cliff Richards, is good to great, the dialogue funny, the plots, well, maybe not brilliant but in the right enough ballpark that it felt authentically like Buffy. ★★★☆☆

City of Stairs

Review by Stephen Theaker

In **City of Stairs** by Robert Jackson Bennett (Broadway
Books (US) and Jo Fletcher Books (UK), ebook, 9396ll)
the cruel, capricious gods have been killed by the
people they oppressed and all the miracles they
performed have been undone, leaving a world that no
longer quite makes sense, and is ruled by their former
slaves, the Saypuri. Bulikov, former capital of the gods'

empire, has been left in a particularly curious state, with transparent walls, staircases that lead nowhere, and other weird anomalies. It is the year 1719 and a Saypuri investigator has taken it upon herself to look into the murder of a friend. Like Columbo, her plain appearance conceals a sharp mind. Dangerously sharp: it's going to get her into a lot of trouble. Bulikov is rife with conspiracies and secrets.

This is a book I loved to bits; it entertains on every level. There is the plot, of course, the mysteries uncovered one by one, the revelations and twists and discoveries. There are echoes of our world – it's a bit like Taiwan and China, a bit UK and India, a bit USA and Mexico – but for a nice change it's not a bit like medieval Europe. At the end of many chapters the reader is simply left dazzled by the pace of events in them – the sheer volume of *cool stuff*. Dead gods, vile monsters, lost kings, fractured realities, politics, oiled-up battles on frozen rivers, sex and hopeless romance – it is rich without ever feeling too much. This is exactly what I want when I read a fantasy novel: a strange new world where thoroughly interesting things are happening. ★★★★☆

Daredevil by Mark Waid, Vol. 1

Review by Stephen Theaker

Mark Waid applies a soft reboot to the Man Without Fear, referencing the dark stories of previous years but permitting Matt Murdock to make a conscious decision to let it go and make a fresh start. Yes, his secret identity made the news, but who believes what they see on the news any more? Taking new cases when there's a media brouhaha is tricky, but Matt and loyal legal partner Foggy Nelson decide to work behind the scenes, coaching litigants in person, and that leads Daredevil into encounters with new enemies. To someone who has read the headline Daredevil stories – like those by Frank Miller, Kevin Smith and Brian Michael Bendis – without digging deep into the back catalogue, this felt like a novel take on the character. Less grubby than usual, with a bright colour palette and a good deal of humour; Daredevil's a supersniffer, so he wants Foggy eating fresh food instead of Wotsits. With its acrobatic and cheerful but still-damaged hero, strong design sense, and science adventure elements, Waid's *Daredevil* is reminiscent of Mike Allred's *Madman*, though it's a bit less poppy and zany. The writing and art are clever and imaginative, the stories showing the many uses to which the blind superhero can put his supersensory powers, and the artists, Marcos Martin and Paolo Rivera, finding many clever ways to show how those powers work – the cover being a good example. It's nice to see Daredevil dragged out of the doldrums and having some fun.

★★★☆☆

Deliver Us from Evil

Review by Douglas J. Ogurek

Demonic possession/police procedural mash-up delivers, but doesn't stand among most hallowed horror films.

A mysterious hooded figure hanging out at a zoo coaxes a woman into attempting to kill her child. So begins an investigation that will call into question Bronx cop Ralph Sarchie's (Eric Bana) faith (or lack thereof) and sanity.

Deliver Us from Evil (2014), directed by Scott

Derrickson, adds a police procedural twist to levitate the film to above par status in the overdone demonic possession subgenre. During Sarchie's journey, the viewer encounters a horde of proven scare tactics: disturbing video footage, creepy wall text and symbols, basement explorations, toys moving on their own, faces and bodies popping onto the screen, and sinister noises.

Sarchie begins to link the zoo incident footage (which calls to mind M. Night Shyamalan's *The Happening* (2008)) to three Iraq War veterans. As Sarchie navigates "the sewer" of his precinct, his findings take a toll. His relationship with his wife and child worsens. He starts to see and hear things that others cannot. An event from his past begins to surface. Then there is the more immediate threat of the hooded figure, who grows more dangerous as Sarchie gets closer to the truth.

Eric Bana, known to many as "the first Hulk" (*Hulk*, 2003), proves a wise casting choice. He offers a hardened cop with a believable lack of introspection. Sarchie's raw protestations against the supernatural add a bit of humour. I'm paraphrasing here: "I hate it when people blame little fairies for all the bad shit they do," or "She didn't try to kill her kid because she's possessed. She tried to kill her kid because she's fuckin' crazy." The concerned expression that Bana has perfected and his New York accent are bonuses.

Funny man Joel McHale of the TV series *Community* plays Sarchie's wise-cracking sidekick Butler. He's the type of guy who wears a Boston Red Sox hat in Yankees territory to see how people will react. One would expect a little more depth from him.

Possessed by Possession Tropes
There really isn't anything groundbreaking about *Deliver Us from Evil*. Still, like a slew of other recent

horror films, especially James Wan films like *Insidious* (2010) and *The Conjuring* (2013), it effectively packages horror film tropes. I was engaged throughout.

One of *Deliver Us from Evil's* greatest strengths is its use of sound. For instance, there are times when Sarchie's flashlight searches – remember, he's a cop so there's a justification for doing so – go silent to ratchet up the tension. Additionally, a leitmotif of static and children's laughter builds and connects with an incident from Sarchie's past.

An invisible entity likes to make noises in Sarchie's daughter's room. Though they are not adequately explained, the loud scratching and her toy owl's unprompted "haha hoo haha hoo" are admirably nerve-racking. And no matter how many times we hear it, the "Pop Goes the Weasel" song that accompanies the jack-in-the-box continues to build tension.

The inevitable exorcism in this film is theatrical and a bit lengthy, yet entertaining in a "how far will they take this?" kind of way. There's even humour: a cop, viewing the event through one-way glass, occasionally makes overly dramatic comments rife with profanity.

Deliver Us from Evil gives a fix to horror aficionados, but they will find its scares short-lived. So continues the quest to outdo the abiding terror that *Paranormal Activity* brought in 2007. ★★★★☆

Glorkian Warrior: The Trials of Glork

Review by Stephen Theaker

I had read in the later volumes of *American Elf* that James Kochalka was working on a video game, but I'd sort of assumed it was going to be a flash game for his publisher's website or something like that. A big surprise then to find that Kochalka and PixelJam's **Glorkian Warrior: The Trials of Glork** (played on iPod Touch 5) is a fully-fledged app store game, and an excellent one at that. It takes the Glorkian Warrior (whose first book *The Glorkian Warrior Delivers a Pizza* was reviewed in TQF#47) and his trusty backpack and gives them room to run and jump around at the bottom of the screen like idiots while waves of invaders attack from above. The backpack constantly shoots, leaving the Glorkian Warrior to worry about dodging bullets, completing missions set by little girl aliens in space armour, and collecting crackers and power-ups. They're the usual type of thing: fireballs, missiles, wiggly bullets, tennis balls. It's all a play on *Space Invaders*, but Kochalka's designs are so appealing and the gameplay so enjoyable that this became that rarest of things: a mobile game I played out of love rather than boredom or dogged determination. It's funny, but fair, death always feeling like it's your own fault, even when the immediate

cause is a Magic Robot who throws exploding birthday
cakes your way. Points and crackers earn upgrades. The
last one, for collecting twenty thousand credits?
Ennui: the Glorkian Warrior begins to look bored if
you stand still. ★★★★☆

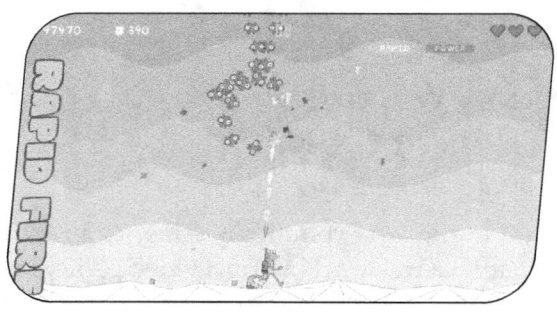

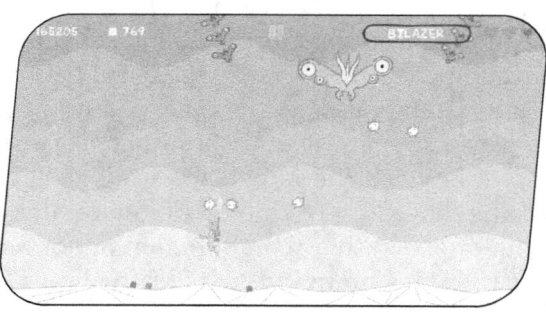

Guardians of the Galaxy

Review by Stephen Theaker

Guardians of the Galaxy (Marvel, 121 mins), directed and co-written by James Gunn, begins with a boy, Peter Quill, saying goodbye to his dying mother. Running in tears from the hospital he is abducted by aliens. It's the beginning of a life of adventure, and that's where we meet him next, a couple of decades later. He's a dumbcracking rascal, going by the name of Star-Lord, on the trail of an ancient relic. So are Yondu Udonta (a merc, his former boss), Ronan the

Accuser, and Nebula and Gamora (the adopted daughters of Thanos). And Star-Lord has two bounty hunters on his own tail: tree-like Groot and Rocket, a cybernetically-enhanced raccoon. After causing a scene on a peaceful planet, Star-Lord, Rocket, Groot and Gamora end up in space prison, where they meet Drax the Destroyer, an implacable enemy of Thanos. At first, the five seem to have little in common, but they will become... the Guardians of the Galaxy!

The original Guardians of the Galaxy stories were set in the 31st century; this film adapts the short-lived Abnett and Lanning series about a present-day group that nicked the name – though the film leaves out Quasar, Mantis and Adam Warlock, and reduces Cosmo the psychic space dog to a non-speaking role. If none of those names mean anything to you, it might seem strange that such a little-known comic has made it to cinemas ahead of, say, the Flash, the Teen Titans, or Wonder Woman, and it is strange, but this isn't a second-string film. The special effects are spectacular, both big (giant spaceships in battle) and small (Groot's glowy spores). The cast plays it with gusto, but they hold tight to the hearts of their characters. The use of music is inspired: Star-Lord's prize possession is a mixtape made by his mum in the eighties, and classic (and some not-so-classic) tracks are dropped into the film at the perfect times. And it has a post-credits scene that left me gobsmacked. Wish I could watch a film like this every week.
★★★★☆

I Killed Rasputin

Review by Stephen Theaker

A film, *I Killed Rasputin* (1967), has been made of the memoir of Prince Felix Yusupov, who claims to have killed Rasputin, the dangerously influential Russian monk. Well, he claims to have kicked off the process with a bit of poisoning, before shooting and drowning finished the tenacious Mad Monk off. Or did it? Was *any* of the story true? An American journalist has his doubts, and comes to interview the elderly Yusupov (played by Nichola McAuliffe), though the prince's wife Irina (a niece of the executed tsar) often chips in. This is the story of **I Killed Rasputin**, a new play by Richard Herring, showing during August at the George Square Theatre as part of the Edinburgh Fringe. It's a very funny piece, cleverly staged – the windows of the prince's apartment double as windows into the past, scenes playing out behind the fog of transparencies. To some extent it's the dramatisation and exposition of a theory, but it's an interesting theory and it works with the characters, illuminating rather than overwhelming them, taking us further into the heart of the foolish man who says he did it. Even now he is plagued by the Mad Monk: the play begins with him seeing off Rasputin once again, this time with a waste basket! Though at first it came as a slight disappointment that Herring wasn't playing Rasputin (I thought that was him in the poster), the cast is excellent, right down to the prince's dog, showing wit and versatility. And though I saw a fairly early show in the run, it felt well-rehearsed, the quick changes passing off without a hitch. I do recommend it, though families should be warned that the 12+ rating it got in the Fringe guide was a bit off – I'd put it at 15 at least, thanks to swearing and simulated (albeit jokey) sex. Otherwise, if you get the chance, be sure to catch this play. ★★★★☆

I Need a Doctor: the Whosical

Review by Stephen Theaker

I Need a Doctor: the Whosical, by Jessica Spray and James Wilson-Taylor, showing as part of the Edinburgh Fringe at the Pleasance Above during August, is a comedic musical starring two performers, Jess and James, whose hopes of staging a Doctor Who show have been thwarted by BBC red tape. Hoped-for guest stars from the Whoniverse have sent their apologies and only the two of them are left. Undeterred, they press on. Jess will play the companion, and James will play everyone else: the Exterminators, Da Masta, Amy Wand, K-10, and *a* doctor (not *the* Doctor), cleverly dodging copyright concerns in an adventure through time and space. The songs are catchy (I even bought the CD), the performances are energetic and joyful, and with jokes about Tennant-fancying and fanlore this works as well for big kids as little ones. ★★★★☆

'ferociously imaginative ... smart, dark, visceral'
LAUREN BEUKES
KAMERON HURLEY
INFIDEL
2012 BRITISH FANTASY AWARD WINNER

Infidel

Review by Tim Atkinson

There's nothing this reviewer better enjoys than returning to an author and finding that they've upped their game. Compared to *God's War*, Kameron Hurley's still striking debut, its sequel *Infidel* is better in every respect.

While the former foundered a little under the weight of its baroque world-building, *Infidel* returns to the same setting to *tell a story*. And by revisiting much the same cast, building on what has gone before, Hurley shows that she can invest these characters with depth and moral complexity.

Infidel's fictional universe resists easy categorisation: Hurley herself suggests *bug-punk*, which is at least pithier than *grimdark-feminist-biotech-anti-clerical-planetary romance*.

But try picturing a crapsack desert planet populated by bloody-minded Abrahamic monotheists: some matriarchal, nearly all of them homicidal. And then throw in the insects. *Lots and lots of insects.*

Once tools of terraforming, colonies of genetically engineered critters are now the basis of the planetary economy of the remote world of Umayma. Transport, medicine, architecture, war: all are powered by bugs manipulated by specially attuned "magicians".

I cannot begin to tell you how much I like this idea.

While its treatment in *Infidel* is pretty much indistinguishable from magic, the concept is SF to the core, extrapolating boldly from the remote-controlled flies of today's laboratories. And for me a real taste of otherness is a fair exchange for some authorial hand-waving.

Having done most of this scene-setting in *God's War*, Hurley kicks the sequel off *in media res* and pushes onwards at a cracking rate, alternating between bloody action and murky intrigue. Our main point-of-view character is Nyx: bounty-hunter, former state-sponsored assassin and all-round toxic individual.

Starting out in the first book as not much more than forward momentum with occasional swearing, she has grown in the sequel to become a tragic protagonist. She is not a nice person by any definition: she murders, tortures and betrays to get her way. But Nyx is a *self-aware monster*; she doesn't like what she's become. She's capable of radical selflessness in her dealings with her team. And she's guided more than she admits by her own residual but strangely irreducible code of honour.

It's her honour and loyalty to her country which led Nyx in *Infidel* to accept an offer to investigate the attempted regicide of her Queen by renegade assassins. In no time at all, she finds herself a barbarian in a foreign country, unexpectedly reunited with former team-mates, out of her depth, double-crossed and played.

All of this makes for a much better constructed plot than *God's War*. Hurley still may be a little too prone to invoking the Coincidence Fairy to tie up the loose ends, but there's a fine thriller underneath all the insectile trappings. And while I honestly still couldn't tell you exactly what the antagonists actually wanted in the first book, here I don't just know their aims, I could even empathise with them to some degree.

Despite being a giant leap forward for the author, the same things "bug" me about *Infidel* as its predecessor. Hurley has impeccable liberal credentials – as anyone who has read her blog will be aware – yet as Adam Roberts has pointed out in an otherwise positive review of *God's War*, writing pseudo-Middle Eastern desert-dwellers intent on killing each other over religious differences is inherently open to problematic readings. And for all that faith is core to the world Hurley has created, there's no sense of why it matters so vitally to its people or fuels global conflict.

Infidel may fall short of greatness, but it's still a very good book. And it's *only her second, people, only her second!* My hopes for *Rapture*, the third in this trilogy, are high indeed.

SCARLETT JOHANSSON   MORGAN FREEMAN

THE AVERAGE PERSON USES 10%
OF THEIR BRAIN CAPACITY.
IMAGINE WHAT SHE COULD DO WITH 100%.

A FILM BY LUC BESSON

LUCY

Lucy

Review by Stephen Theaker

Sorry to say it, but **Lucy** would be a better film if
Morgan Freeman's scenes were cut. It's no fault of the
actor: his character's lecture on accessing the full
potential of the human brain is so daft that if I'd been
watching on TV I'd have changed the channel. In the
cinema, I got through it by deciding that this film
takes place on an Earth where animals really do use
only a few percentage points of their brains – though

why would evolution encourage them to do so? – and human brains are similarly wasted.

Until Lucy, that is, who while being forced to act as a drug mule gets kicked in the belly, making an experimental drug leak into her system. It's an artificial replication of the substance that lets a foetus develop so quickly in a mother's womb, and the effect on Lucy is to cause all the cells in her body to be replaced at an incredible rate, letting her "colonise" her own brain and acquire incredible powers.

Super-strength and super-intelligence come first, then later telekinesis, mind control, changing her physical appearance, and tapping into electronic communications. By the end she can do pretty much everything she sets her mind to, apart from, apparently, dealing adequately with the gangsters who want their drugs back, leading to a bloody massacre of the police protecting the university laboratory where Lucy tries to save herself.

Lucy would be a typical film from the Luc Besson European action factory, another in the line of *The Transporter*, *Unleashed* and *Taken*, all guns, gangsters and car chases, but it's a bit better than that for two reasons: the science fiction angle, because although the science is ludicrous, the powers in action are great fun; and Scarlett Johansson, who is compelling and committed, giving an Oscar-level performance in a film that seems surprised to contain it.

Not bad, but don't take 100% of your brain to the cinema. ★★★☆☆

The Making of Star Wars

Review by Jacob Edwards

A mile-long star ship, an alien cantina and a dogfight in space. Everything else is detail.

Anybody who by 1977 had been associated with SF being made for either the small or the big screen would attest that *Star Wars* (later subtitled: *A New Hope*) changed everything. It is perhaps difficult to appreciate the enormity of *Star Wars'* impact in retrospect of all the flashy SF and CGI-driven fluff that has come after – one would have to judge the movie only in the context of filmmaking to that point in time; which, like requiring a jury to disregard evidence, is asking the impossible – but even those who were born too late to experience *Star Wars* upon its original cinematic release perhaps will have found themselves drawn into watching it on DVD (often several times) or habitually whensoever it is shown on television, commercials and all. The franchise nowadays is taken for granted, as are the visual effects for which *Star Wars* was the forerunner, yet in its day the movie was an unprecedented phenomenon – as suddenly huge as it was unexpected – and weighing in at 362 large, glossy pages (28cm x 26cm), the majority of which are resplendent with production photographs, artwork and designs, J.W. Rinzler's **The Making of Star Wars** (Aurum Press, 362pp; 2013; first published: Ebury Press, 2007) both establishes the cinematic milieu in which George Lucas's film was made and goes a long way towards fostering an appreciation of its significance. Drawing for the most part on rediscovered interviews that Lucasfilm vice-president Charles Lippincott had conducted between 1975 and 1978 for a "making of..." book that went unwritten, Rinzler promises his readers a host of contemporaneous recollections and thence the definitive account of *Star Wars* both as it unfolded and as it was perceived shortly after completion, before the effects of its trailblazing became fully evident: in other words, the inside story of a history that was still very much in the making.

For all that the finished product proved to be of lasting consequence, *Star Wars* had a troubled genesis both creatively and in terms of George Lucas's strained working relationship with Hollywood and the studio system. Lucas had enormous difficulty developing and explicating his grand concept, and much though 20th Century Fox might come across as short-sighted and unreasonable in its dealings, this is the one instance in which Rinzler has allowed his exposé to carry a selective bias, the pro-*Star Wars* effusiveness of his source material resulting in a favouring of the film's historical success over what may well have been quite valid concerns on Fox's part. Lucas himself is treated in more balanced a fashion, and emerges as a quintessentially independent filmmaker attempting through sheer force of will to exert control over every aspect of a gargantuan undertaking, not so much because he was obsessive/possessive (although clearly he was) but because the intricacies of the movie, in combination with its epic and ambitious scale, necessitated that each component have its requirements and problems attended to in minutiae by people who worked in artistic isolation, glimpsing only a sliver of Lucas's overarching visualisation until such time as *Star Wars* was fully realised and came to be shown on the big screen. George Lucas knew exactly what he wanted – his orchestrating of talents calls to mind Brian Wilson, who would compose Beach Boys songs in his head and assign parts to each member of the group, the tunes then emerging fully formed – but while Lucas shaped every nuance and every frame of *Star Wars*, other people nevertheless made seminal contributions, and the constraints of time and budget also played their part in determining what was achievable. Furthermore, Lucas's absolute purity and exactitude of vision would come to the fore only after several (at times nebulous) globules of creativity had coalesced to the point of registering on his internal scanner of certitude and so becoming part of the production process. Fans who live and breathe *Star Wars* through a continuity filter they cannot suffer to remove should remember that much of the detail they now hold as sacrosanct, Lucas patched together over many years to accommodate nothing more *de rigueur* than a broad reenergising of the space opera genre and two or three set piece scenes he thought would be visually effective. Darth Vader's iconic mask was originally part of a spacesuit, not a core element of his character. The Millennium Falcon took on its distinctive shape as a hasty revision after there appeared on *Space: 1999* a ship too much like the model already built. Luke in one draft was a woman, and only at the eleventh hour was renamed Skywalker (from Starkiller, which was thought to evince A-list celebrity murders). Even something as seemingly quintessential as Obi-Wan Kenobi's demise aboard the Death Star was a late script change, concocted during filming and (at least in its initial form) to the disgruntlement of Sir Alec Guinness.

While making *Star Wars* George Lucas demanded something akin to godlike autonomy within a constantly evolving framework – almost as if directing a lucid dream – and in examining each scene of the movie from conception to final edit, *The Making of Star Wars* shows not only how particular he was in piecing together his magnum opus, but also, oddly, how malleable the *Star Wars* universe proved in its formative stages and how very different each element could have been. The movie that is so greatly beloved by audiences in fact fell well short of what Lucas had hoped to achieve, and throughout pre-production, filming and then post-production he consistently expressed his disappointment: so much so that amidst the cornucopia of production photos in Rinzler's book – an invaluable visual record and an idiosyncratic time capsule of 1970s fashion – it is difficult to look upon Lucas's bearded, curly haired, frustrated visage and not construe a harbinger of Rowan Atkinson's oft-thwarted Elizabethan incarnation of Blackadder. Such nefarious associations aside, the lush and unstinting pictorial content ensures that *The Making of Star Wars* is well worth delving into as a coffee table book, albeit one that retails at £40.00 and contains matter-of-fact prose sufficiently exhaustive to constitute heavy reading for even the most dedicated of fans. From the technical side of filmmaking it is hard to envisage a more comprehensive work, but Rinzler's compendium is valuable beyond its dry chronicling of method and fact, offering much also by way of anecdote and in

bringing out the personalities of those people
(particularly Lucas) who dedicated themselves to the
making of *Star Wars*.

All told, Rinzler's is a book that should appeal to
anyone with a fondness for *Star Wars* or an interest in
the history and development of SF motion pictures.
The question of whether or not it's worth the cover
price might fall ultimately to such intangibles as how
badly you'd like to meet the walrus who voiced
Chewbacca, or how curious you are as to how a bantha
may be brought to life sans CGI but one elephant to
the good. If nothing else, though, *The Making of Star
Wars* constitutes an unparalleled vista of behind-the-
scenes enterprise, and for most of us an eye-opener as
to the vast quantities of time, money and effort poured
into each labyrinthine second of screen time on a
science fiction classic such as that which Lucas
delivered unto the world in the cinematic dawn of
1977.

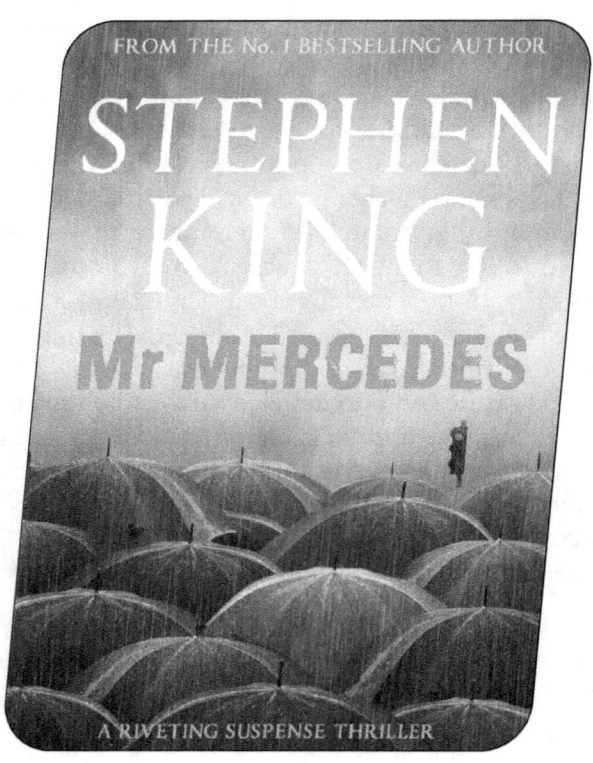

Mr Mercedes

Review by Rafe McGregor

In June 1999 Stephen King was run over by a Dodge
minivan while on his daily four-mile walk. Three years
later, he was still unable to sit down for long periods
without severe pain and announced his intention to
stop writing. Eight years later, he wrote that "the force
of my invention has slowed down a lot", a tragic
admission for a prolific author whose work has ranged
across the horror, science fiction, fantasy, crime, and
thriller genres. **Mr Mercedes** (Hodder & Stoughton,
416pp) is King's sixth full-length novel since his

accident. Like some of his best work – *Rita Hayworth and Shawshank Redemption* (1982) and *Misery* (1987) to name but two – there is no supernatural element at play and the narrative follows a retired detective's attempt to catch a spree killer before he strikes again. Like *Duma Key* (2008), the novel is subdivided into very short numbered sections and the eight named parts are really chapters, varying from one to forty-three sub-sections each, which (a few excepted) tell the tale from either the protagonist or antagonist's point of view.

Mr Mercedes does not plumb the existential depths of *Rita Hayworth and Shawshank Redemption*, nor is it likely to have the popular appeal of *The Stand* (1978) or *The Shining* (1977), but it isn't the work of a writer whose inventive force is flagging either. From the dramatic yet restrained opening, in which a grey Mercedes emerges from the fog in as frightening a manner as any mythical monster, to the plausible handling of the various plot twists, there is no evidence that King's creativity is on the wane. Perhaps the most interesting aspect of *Mr Mercedes* is its *intra*-textuality, King's explicit and implicit references to works previous and forthcoming, with recurring symbols and motifs from his extensive oeuvre. The murder weapon recalls, of course, both *Christine* (1983) and *From a Buick 8* (2002) and the killer's disguises as a clown and ice cream vendor, *It* (1986). The final stage of the story, which places the detective in an unlikely trio of crime-fighters, is reminiscent of *The Dark Tower* series (eight books published from 1982 to 2012). There are also at least two allusions to *Revival*, King's next novel, which is due for publication in November. *Mr Mercedes* is, to some extent, a homage to King's own work, but with such an illustrious career upon which to draw, the gesture is long overdue rather than self-indulgent.

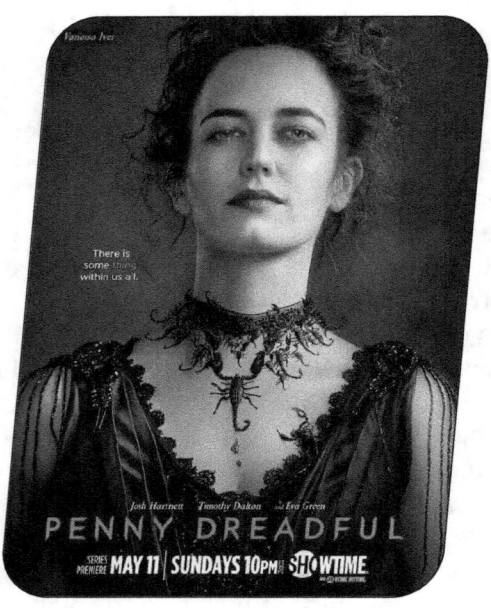

Penny Dreadful, Season 1

Review by Stephen Theaker

Penny Dreadful is a new television take on an old
idea: the out-of-copyright crossover. Here we have
young Doctor Frankenstein (Harry Treadaway) and his
monster (a marvellously melodramatic Rory Kinnear);
Sir Malcolm Murray (Timothy Dalton), father of Mina;
and Dorian Gray (Reeve Carney); plus four apparently
unfamiliar characters: Josh Hartnett as gunslinger
Ethan Chandler; Billie Piper as Brona Croft, the dying
prostitute he falls for; Danny Sapani as Murray's
fighting manservant, Sembene; and Eva Green as
Vanessa Ives, whose prim comportment conceals an
ongoing inner battle with the forces of darkness.

The plot of this first series is driven by Murray's
attempts to rescue his daughter Mina from Dracula.

The cowboy's pistols come in handy as they root out vampire nests, and when the fighting is done Doctor Frankenstein performs autopsies on the monsters' bodies. As the series proceeds, there are complications. Dorian Gray works his seductive way through the cast. Frankenstein's creation demands a bride. Vanessa Ives begins to lose control of her dark passenger, but without its gifts Murray would never find his daughter.

This is a well-made series that I probably wouldn't have watched to the end were it not for Eva Green's gob-smacking performance; in control she's riveting, out of control terrifying. The production values are exceptional, and the special effects terrific, but there is little pay-off on the storylines, too much being held back for a second series that might never have come (though we know now that it will). The vampires are a bit too easy to kill, and seem disinclined to bite; their grand plan is a bit hopeless. Season two will need more compelling antagonists.

Brilliant moments, but not yet a brilliant programme. ★★★☆☆

Return to Armageddon

Review by Stephen Theaker

In **Return to Armageddon** (2000 AD, tpb, 148pp)
spacers find the frozen corpse of the devil on the other
side of a deep space anomaly. As you'd expect of any
mad scientist worth his salt, the on-board doctor
extracts cells to create a clone. Or was it two clones?
Two babies are found with the doctor's dead body, one
cute as a button, the other with black wings and
cloven hooves – the Destroyer! The dead are soon
walking the spaceship's corridors, and that's just the
beginning of a story that ends up with Earth under the
devil's rule, humanity nothing but the squealing meat
of Satan's servants.

This strip by writer Malcolm Shaw and artist Jesus
Redondo (with two episodes drawn by Johnny
Johnson) began in *2000 AD*'s third year of publication,
and ran continuously from issue 185 to 218. It's the
kind of thing that made *2000 AD Extreme Edition* one
of my favourite comics: a self-contained adventure
story I'd never read before. It is a serial through and
through, its only concern to make every episode the
most gobsmacking yet, unceremoniously discarding
characters and plotlines the second they've outlived
their usefulness.

And like so many other stories from *2000 AD*'s early
days, reading it left me gutted that I wasn't reading
this stuff when it came out (though the *Eagle* and
Doctor Who Weekly were good too). I would have
loved its gleeful goriness and boyish malice towards its
own characters. This is a comic for kids in which the
hero – who spends much of the story as a miserable
unkillable monster – returns to Earth after a thirty-
year absence to find the oceans are now "vast
cauldrons of boiling oil" full of people, and both sides
of the planet are in perpetual darkness, the only light
"coming from burning corpses". Kids love that stuff.
Me too. ★★★☆☆

The Seventh Miss Hatfield

Review by Stephen Theaker

The Seventh Miss Hatfield (Gollancz, ebook, 3320ll)
is a novel by Anna Caltabiano, suitable for young
teenagers, about a young woman who impersonates
the niece of Mr Beauford, a wealthy steel magnate, in
order to steal one of his paintings. The year is 1904.
While undercover she begins to fall for the steel
magnate's son, Henley, who quickly rumbles her as an
imposter, and what was originally planned as a quick
theft turns into a months-long stay. Handsome Henley
is promised in marriage to another, the vain and proud
Christine Porter, and though the thief knows she

cannot stay, and certainly cannot marry the man, the thought of separation is breaking both of their hearts.

So why, you might be asking (and probably not for the first time), is this book being reviewed here? Because it's being sold as a literary fantasy, rather than a historical romance. Look at that lovely cover. I expected a literary modern fantasy in the vein of *The Rabbit Back Literature Society*, but got instead a book that would have been too tame and unadventurous for my children.

There is a fantasy twist to the story sketched out above. The indolent thief begins the book as Cynthia, an eleven-year-old girl in 1954, who upon visiting the home of the mysterious Miss Hatfield (sixth of that name) is dosed with a drop of the elixir of life, turning Cynthia into the seventh Miss Hatfield. Now eternal, barring accidents, they have the ability to travel in time, and the sixth Miss Hatfield uses that to age her successor to adulthood. Before the former Cynthia can get on with the fun of being a time-travelling eternal, Miss Hatfield number six has a little job for her: the painting theft mentioned above.

It takes a conversation that lasts almost a fifth of the book to get to that point, and from then on we are into romance territory, where the only real nods to time travel are that number seven has a slightly poorly tummy, which gets worse the longer she stays in the past. This is used in an attempt to add a bit of urgency to the proceedings, albeit with unintentionally comic effect as number seven mentions it, then casually notes another week or three having gone by. It doesn't help that our protagonist isn't worthy of that label. She is slow to act, inertia her primary characteristic. If she were a *Doctor Who* companion every episode would last a fortnight. All she needs to do is steal a painting, or even destroy it – there's no need at all for her to spend months waiting for the right opportunity.

She doesn't seem to worry too much about number six's strange actions towards her, and just follows her orders. She is exceptionally callow and selfish, being for example quite happy to let everyone (including Mr Beauford himself) think Mr Beauford is a lunatic when she knows full well he is not, just in case. She sets great store on being polite to Mr Beauford's servants, but doesn't worry too much about the overall unfairness of a system that would leave a young woman being grateful to receive the scrapings from her plate.

Maybe that's down to Cynthia's original age, but the book doesn't make that explicit. The way that she is a eleven-year-old in a twenty-five-year-old body could potentially have been interesting, though that potential has been explored previously in films like *Big* and *Freaky Friday*, but the book shows no interest in this. There is no sign here that adult relationships are any different to those of eleven-year-olds. Cynthia grows up in a flash, but the book doesn't explore what she has missed in the interim. You can't help thinking that if the book wanted a grown-up main character, it might as well have started with one.

This is a below average book that feels as if it is being pitched to quite the wrong audience. As a novel for young teenagers it might find an appreciative audience, but as a literary fantasy novel for adults it's some way out of its depth. The afterword explains that the author was seventeen when she wrote this. I'd have been very proud to write a book as good as this when I was that age (or indeed at any age), but, unfair as it is, it's hard not to read that and think, right, okay, that probably explains why the book is the way that it is.
★★☆☆☆

The Spectral Link
Review by Rafe McGregor

If Thomas Ligotti is not the *only* contemporary practitioner of weird fiction, the genre that emerged as an epiphenomenon of literary modernism, then he is certainly the most accomplished. This slim volume of his, **The Spectral Link** (Subterranean Press, 94pp), comprises a two-page preface and a pair of short stories which, like his entire oeuvre to date, resist interpretation and exemplify the recondite. Ligotti's acquaintance with the perennial problems of the disciplines constituting the Western tradition of philosophy – logic, metaphysics, epistemology, and ethics – is striking and his work exploits the failure of repeated attempts to answer crucial questions about existence, knowledge, and morality. The suicidal narrator of "Metaphysica Morum" might be speaking for the author when he registers his "scorn for the saved and their smug sense of how perfectly right things were in the universe" because Ligotti appears convinced that all is *not* right in the universe and continually revisits the fearful consequences of this conviction in his strange, singular, uncanny stories. There is a strong impression, for example, that "Metaphysica Morum" is nothing more than a slow, sustained unravelling of the meaning of the word "demoralization", which is exposed as having implications beyond personal concerns with the terminal.

Despite its innocuous title "The Small People" is perhaps the more philosophical of the two tales, exploring one of the most pervasive questions in metaphysics, the difference – if any – between things as they really are and things as we perceive them; or, alternatively, the extent to which human concepts reflect the reality of the natural world. Here, the narrator finds disturbing evidence of a mismatch and realises that he is one of the few possessed of "a type of instinct that actually *forced* me to see things as they were and not as I was supposed to see them so that I could get by in life". He experiences a systematic disintegration of reality when the "small country" he perceives is contrasted first with the "normal country" and then the "big country" until the border between small and big is breached by "halfers". If neither "small" nor "big" map on to the world, do "self" and "other"? As the narrator penetrates deeper into the mystery of small and half-small people, he is less and less able to "get by" and runs the risk of that ultimate undoing... demoralization. Ligotti is a writer of *weird* tales and these two will not be to everyone's taste: their weirdness overflows and unsettles.

Turbulence

Review by Stephen Theaker

Turbulence by Samit Basu (digital audiobook, Audible Ltd, 10 hrs 18 mins) is read by Ramon Tikaram, so, of course, having theoretically appeared in one of his sister's music videos I was well disposed towards it from the off. Vir Singh, a young Indian pilot, has acquired super-powers, and as the novel begins we meet him flying through the air on his way to interfere with Pakistan's nuclear weapons programme. He is not the only one with new powers. Everyone Uzma meets falls in love with her, and she hopes to parlay that into a film career. Aman, a young man who can interface directly with the internet; Narayan, a scientist who builds mad devices in his sleep; Tia, a duplicate-triplicate-infinite girl, and so on. (Apologies for any spelling mistakes – names are always tricky when reviewing an audiobook.) All must come together to fight Jai, a soldier who, like all the others, got exactly what he wanted, from whoever or whatever it was that gave them these powers: for Jai, that was to be the perfect soldier, powerful and indestructible.

Heroes feels like a big influence – of course *Heroes* borrowed its plots from a hundred different comic books itself (the writers even talked about how little work they got done on new comics day!) – but it's the approach that feels so similar. With an audiobook it can sometimes be hard to tell if it's the tone of the book that's odd, or the tone of the reading: here, the mood seems to change from sentence to sentence – serious, quirky, foreboding, fun – making it hard to get a sense of the novel. Ramon Tikaram doesn't seem to be taking it entirely seriously. The result is that, at least in audio form, it felt more cheesy blockbuster than serious science fiction. It's okay, but still a bit of a disappointment. ★★★☆☆

The Violent Century

Review by Tim Atkinson

What's the point of a text-only graphic novel?

I've enjoyed a few superhero stories in recent years – Austin Grossman's *Soon I Will Be Invincible* being a good example. Yet I find they share a common problem: they try to tell the Pop Art tales of their greatest influences with solid but conservative prose. Competing with comics on comics' terms, they're always bound to pull up short.

And this is speculative fiction we're talking about here – chock full of mind-melting ideas and techniques half-inched from serious literature, underway well before Superman was a twinkle in Jerry Siegel and Joe Shuster's eyes.

A good superhero novel should then draw strength from the novelistic tradition at least as much as from its forebears in the funny papers. Lavie Tidhar's *The Violent Century* goes at least some way towards demonstrating this point.

Central to the novel is the idea that, while American costumed crime-fighters, Nazi Ubermenschen and Soviet champions of the proletariat clashed in public, Britain trained its special talents instead as secret agents and players in the great game of espionage.

As the novel opens in the present, Fogg, a telekinetic British operative long since retired, is recalled by an old comrade for one final debrief on an unresolved matter dating back to the end of WW2. His interrogation frames stories of adventure, horror, love and collusion across enemy lines from the past – each revealing more of the real reason for his summons.

Since it draws on war stories and Cold War thrillers more than it does Marvel and DC, *The Violent Century* sidesteps the anxiety of influence affecting previous superhero novels. Despite a few sly references to Stan Lee and Siegel and Shuster, it's confidently its own work.

While reading the novel is an intensely visual experience, the movie in your head is less *Avengers Assemble*, more *Inglourious Basterds*. Tidhar shows himself to be master of the tone needed, writing vignette after vignette from the battlefields of Europe.

Using the tropes of spy novels also allows an altogether more pessimistic take on the uses and abuses of power than you'd normally find in a four-colour universe. As you might expect, Fogg and his fellow British spies owe more to George Smiley than to Nick Fury, but the costumed heroes with which they coexist are not one whit less morally compromised.

Beating the Nazis and the Soviets – the book suggests – comes at the cost of gradually sacrificing one's own principles.

Does *The Violent Century* make the case for the superhero novel as something with real merit in its own right? For me, it's a resounding maybe; since the book makes most sense as a stylistic exercise, a playful what-if, rather than something with serious intent behind it, in practice it lends support to either view.

Yet while it might not be the return favour that superhero comics still owes literature for *Watchmen*, it is fun, fast and deeply atmospheric. I'm glad that *The Violent Century* exists as a novel, rather than being confined to panels and speech bubbles.

And that, at least, is progress.

World of Fire

Review by Stephen Theaker

Dev Harmer has a new body, not for the first time: this one is heavyset and muscular, with nocturnal vision and hyper-efficient thermoregulation. Dev is a troubleshooter, sent by Interstellar Security Solutions wherever needed to combat the sneaky attacks of the machines. The overt war is over, but the covert one continues, as atheist Earth battles the religious AIs of Polis+ for control of vital resources. Dev died in that war, but his consciousness was saved and now this is his life, hopping from one body to another in hopes of eventually earning a new one to call his own.

This time Dev has been sent to Calder's Edge, a sweltering hot mining colony on Alighieri – hence the body modifications – and as soon as he arrives someone tries to blow him up. From then on it's one thrill after another as he tries to uncover the cause of the earthquakes that are making the miners and colonists think about leaving for safer working environments. There are giant man-eating worms, brainwashed scientists, runaway trains and a local chief of police, Captain Kahlc, who won't give him the time of day till he proves he's not just another one of her problems.

I read this on holiday and it was perfect for kicking back. It's something of a throwback to the likes of Dumarest and James Bond, where a tough dude gets chucked into a tough new situation and fights his way out of it, albeit with a more enlightened approach to its female characters. I'm guessing a story arc will develop over the series (as it did in Dumarest), but if in the unlikely event I never read another of Dev's adventures this one was completely satisfying on its own. ★★★★☆

Yesterday's Kin

Review by Stephen Theaker

Dr Marianne Jenner has discovered the thirty-first group of humans sharing a haplogroup of mitochondrial DNA, and though she's very pleased to have done so it's hardly the sort of thing that would explain her invitation to the Embassy, the mysterious home to the unseen aliens recently arrived on Earth. She'll find out that the people of both planets share a common enemy, and potentially a common doom, and have much more in common besides. A major theme of **Yesterday's Kin** (Tachyon Publications, pb, 192pp) is family, and Jenner has plenty of trouble with hers. Her husband died fifteen years ago, her three children are at loggerheads with each other and her. The youngest, Noah, habitual user of mind-swapping drug sugarcane, will also end up on the Embassy, though that'll do little to bring mother and child any closer together. This is the kind of novel I thought they didn't make any more. Short, but complete in itself, giving clever scientists an intractable problem and an impossible deadline. A fascinating alien culture, psychological insight into our own. And what seems like (to this non-scientist, at least) real science. It's not a horror story, or a western, or a war story dressed in space clothes, but proper full-blooded science fiction, and I loved it. I get the feeling that I will be reading many more books by Nancy Kress. ★★★★☆

Also Received, But Not Yet Reviewed

Notes by Stephen Theaker

Ashley, Allen and Sarah Doyle, *Dreaming Spheres: Poems of the Solar System* (PS Publishing)

Bassen, L.S., *Summer of the Long Knives* (Signal 8 Press)

Brown, Eric, *Sacrifice on Spica III* (PS Publishing)

Brown, Timothy, *Polaris* (PS Publishing): a novella

Campbell, Ramsey, *Think Yourself Lucky* (PS Publishing): a new novel

Connell, Brendan, *The Metanatural Adventures of Dr. Black* (PS Publishing): looks very interesting

Ellis, Peter Berresford, *The Shadow of Mr Vivian* (PS Publishing): a biography of E. Charles Vivian, also known as Jack Mann

Farrell, Kate, *My Name is Mary Sutherland* (PS Publishing): a novel

Guffey, Robert, *Spies and Saucers* (PS Publishing): three novellas

Hale, Edward Everett, and Adam Roberts, *The Brick Moon* (Jurassic London)

Hines, Jim C., *Codex Born* (Del Rey)

Hodder, Mark, *The Return of the Discontinued Man* (Del Rey): fifth in the Burton and Swinburne series; came with the paperback of previous entry *The Secret of Abdu el Yezdi*

Hodder, Mark, *The Silent Thunder Caper* (Obverse Books): first in a new series of Sexton Blake adventures. Also includes a reprint, *The Wireless Telephone Clue* by G.H. Teed.

Hughes, Matthew, *Of Whimsies and Noubles* (PS Publishing): a third Luff Imbry novella from PS

Johnston, John J., and Jared Shurin (eds), *Unearthed* (Jurassic London)

Kernot, David (ed.), *Andromeda Spaceways Inflight Magazine #59*

Kochalka, James, *The Glorkian Warrior Eats Adventure Pie* (First Second)

Lavender III, Isiah, *Black and Brown Planets: The Politics of Race in Science Fiction* (University Press of Mississippi): my review of this interesting book will probably appear in *Interzone* #255

Lebbon, Tim, *Shifting of Veils* (PS Publishing): the third novella in the Apocalypse trilogy

Mann, George, *Doctor Who: Engines of War* (Broadway Books): very excited about reading this, the first novel about the mysterious War Doctor, as played on screen by John Hurt

Morris, Mark, *The Black* (PS Publishing): a novel

Pflug, Ursula, *Harvesting the Moon* (PS Publishing): a collection of short stories

Schwarz, Liesel, *A Clockwork Heart* (Del Rey): second in The Chronicles of Light and Shadow; see #43 for a review of the first, *A Conspiracy of Alchemists*

Schwarz, Liesel, *Sky Pirates* (Del Rey): third in The Chronicles of Light and Shadow; I didn't enjoy the first one enough to read the follow-ups, but they are good-looking books

Shurin, Jared (ed.), *Irregularity* (Jurassic London)

Shurin, Jared (ed.), *The Book of the Dead* (Jurassic London)

Sullivan, Tricia, *Shadowboxer* (Ravenstone)

Tallerman, David, *Prince Thief* (Angry Robot): the latest book in the Easie Damasco series

Unsworth, Simon Kurt, *Strange Gateways* (PS Publishing): a collection of short stories

Wagner, John, and friends, *Judge Dredd: The Complete Case Files 23* (2000AD)

Whiteley, Aliya, *The Beauty* (Unsung Stories): an excellent novella; my review appeared in *Interzone* #254

Williams, Tad, *Sleeping Late on Judgement Day* (Hodder & Stoughton)

Forthcoming Attractions

Expect **Theaker's Quarterly Fiction #50** round about Christmas. Deadline for submissions is **November 31**. We're hoping to make this one a celebration of all that's gone before, so we'd love to hear from past contributors.

Most weeks begin with a new review on our blog: **www.theakersquarterly.blogspot.com**

Stephen tweets every few days or so at: **www.twitter.com/Rolnikov**

Our email address is: **theakersquarterlyfiction@gmail.com**